BLACK DAHLIA

TIFFANY PATTERSON

TMP PUBLISHING LLC

PROLOGUE

Mercedes stared into the most piercing brown eyes she'd ever seen. They belonged to Raul Santiago, the best friend of her best friend's husband. The pair had been partnered together as best man and maid of honor at the wedding.

Now that the night was coming to an end, Mercedes was tired of the flirtation. She was more interested in finding out if Raul could deliver on the promise held in his gaze whenever he looked her way.

"Are you going to finally take me up to your room or what?" she asked as Raul held her pressed against his firm body. His six-two frame towered over her five-foot-nine height even in the four-inch stiletto heels she wore.

The golden skin around Raul's brown eyes wrinkled when his pink lips spread into a knowing smile. Mercedes' stomach muscles tightened at the sight of that grin. Raul was a beautiful man with his striking medium golden skin thanks to his Brazilian heritage, angular jaw, and almost jet-black hair.

What struck Mercedes the most about Raul's features was the intense magnitude of his stare. Whenever he looked at her, Mercedes felt a pull toward him that she couldn't ignore, try as she might.

Raul dipped his head so his lips hovered just above Mercedes'. "Is that what you want?" he asked in a low, seductive tone.

Mercedes lowered her gaze to his mouth, which was so close to her own, and unconsciously licked her lips. Closing her eyes, she bit her bottom lip to prevent a moan.

Raul's hand tightened around her waist, pulling her even deeper into his hold.

While her eyes remained closed, she felt the lightest touch of soft lips to the corner of her mouth. Mercedes had her answer to his question. Opening her eyes, she nodded. "More than anything."

Pleased with her response, Raul moved quickly, as he started to guide her out of the reception toward the elevator. As soon as the elevator doors opened, he pulled Mercedes inside and pushed the button for the top floor, where his rented suite was located.

Using his body, Raul pressed Mercedes' back into the elevator wall. She was in the perfect position to wrap her arms around his neck and bring his head down for a kiss. But just before their lips touched, Raul paused to stare into her eyes, as if searching for something.

He held onto her chin with his free hand as he observed her. The coloring in his eyes deepened, a renewed hunger entering them.

The scorching look he gave her made Mercedes' belly flip flop. Raul slowly lowered his head, sticking his tongue out to lick Mercedes' plump bottom lip. He nipped at her lip, before sucking it into his mouth and licking it to soothe the bite.

Raul moved in for a full kiss. While his lips and tongue assaulted her mouth, he let his strong hands move down Mercedes' waist and stroke her thighs. After deftly finding the end of Mercedes' bridesmaid's dress, he rolled the ends up to caress her smooth, dark brown thighs.

Mercedes' breasts ached from the growing need in her body. Pressing her chest into Raul's body, she pulled him in even closer when she felt his hands glide up her thighs to rub her ass. She made a mental note to thank Devyn for choosing the shorter bridesmaids' dresses, instead of the floor-length gowns her friend had originally wanted.

Easy access is the gift that keeps on giving, she thought when she felt Raul's hand maneuvering around to the front to cup her panty-covered mound.

Raul's lips trailed from her mouth to kiss her jawline, and down her neck, nipping and sucking as he went. He was so caught up in the feel of her beneath his hands and lips, and her breasts pressing into his chest, that he nearly missed the ding of the elevator.

They reluctantly pulled apart, staring at one another. Both were stunned by the amount of chemistry between them. Despite having their fair share of lovers in the past, experiencing this level of desire, so soon after meeting was new for either one.

"We're here," Raul said. He brushed his lips over Mercedes' again, unable to keep his mouth off of her body for too long.

"Mmmm, 'bout time," she moaned.

Raul grabbed Mercedes' hand, pulling her off the elevator, and quickly made his way down the hall to his suite. Once they reached his door, Raul's urgent need to feel Mercedes in his arms again got to him.

He felt like he was possessed with his mounting desire for this woman.

He spun her around so that her back pressed into the door behind her, and greedily took her lips in another possessive kiss. For long moments they stood outside of his suite, allowing their hands and mouths to do the talking. With Raul's lips on her neck, Mercedes moved her hand over the front of his tailored tuxedo to cup his erection.

Impressed would be an understatement for how Mercedes felt as she stroked his large cock through his pants.

"Querida." Raul's voice sounded husky, thick with his need for the woman in his arms.

He continued to pepper kisses along her jawline, allowing his hands to move around to grip her firm backside. The only sounds that could be heard were the small moans coming from Mercedes' mouth, and the words of endearment, mostly in Raul's native, Portuguese.

Finally, Raul forced himself to separate their bodies so that he could remove his key card from his pocket.

Mercedes took in his eyes, lidded heavily with desire, and his slightly swollen lips. She imagined his face was a mirror of her own desire. Opening the door, Raul moved to the side to allow Mercedes entrance.

Within seconds of stepping into the room, Mercedes knew something was wrong. Two feet from the door were a pair of women's high-heeled shoes. Farther inside of the suite a red dress was strewn on the carpet.

Mercedes continued to follow the clothing trail until her eyes landed on a woman, laying completely nude on the suite's couch.

"What the fuck?" Raul's voice boomed from behind Mercedes.

"What is this?" Mercedes asked incredulously.

Raul ignored Mercedes' question and focused on the naked woman who appeared shocked at seeing them both standing there. His face was a mask of anger. "Cindy, what the fuck are you doing in my suite?"

Cindy stood up from the couch without bothering to cover herself. "I thought since we seemed to have a connection downstairs, we could bring the party to your room. I'm not opposed to threesomes," she said, looking at Mercedes, and then back to Raul.

"Girl, you wish." Mercedes rolled her eyes before turning to Raul. "Is this what you planned? For us to have a threesome with some floozy I don't even know?"

She should've known. Men who looked like Raul Santiago were all the same. Manwhores, who only wanted one thing. Which, ordinarily, was fine with Mercedes, since she wasn't looking for anything serious. But for him to think she would agree to something like this without even checking with her first was too much for her.

Mercedes didn't wait for Raul to answer, she began retreating to the door. Raul's hand on her arm stopped her.

"This was not my idea at all. I barely know this woman." There was a hard edge to Raul's tone as he glared back at the still-naked woman.

But Mercedes didn't care to hear his excuses. She was aware of how men lie, cheat, and play Mr. Innocent when caught red-handed.

She wasn't about to be a fool for any man.

"Whatever. I don't have time for this. I'm leaving," she huffed, and snatched her arm out of his grip. The intense yearning she'd felt just moments before had completely fizzled out, replaced by ire.

Mercedes heard Cindy call Raul's name as she exited the suite.

Mercedes contemplated taking the stairs to get away from Raul, but they were on the twenty-fifth floor, and she was in four-inch stilettos. Before she could even make it to the elevator, Raul caught up with her.

"Wait. This is not what it looks like," Raul tried to explain.

"Leave me alone and go back to your girlfriend or whoever the hell she is!" Mercedes snapped.

"She's *not* my girlfriend. I barely know her."

"I don't care," Mercedes interjected with a wave of her hand. "This was a mistake anyway. I'm going home."

She didn't even turn to look over her shoulder at Raul, but she heard his loud sigh, just as the elevator doors opened. She quickly stepped on the elevator and pressed the button for the ground floor, only turning around once the doors closed.

On the elevator ride down, Mercedes chastised herself for feeling as angry as she was. She didn't know Raul. He wasn't her man, or even in the potential running to be her man. They were part of a wedding party, hooking up for the night.

So why was she so angry that he had someone else waiting for him in his room?

As Mercedes stepped off the elevator, she was greeted by Lorenzo, a stern-looking man, whom she knew was working security for Devyn and Nikola's wedding.

"Hello, Ms. Holmes. Mr. Santiago asked me to be your escort home," he said, managing a half smile.

"Excuse me?" she asked, still angry.

"Mr. Santiago asked me to make sure you got home safely. I have the car right out front."

"You work for Rau— Mr. Santiago?" she asked, recalling that Devyn did mention something about Raul working in security.

"Yes, ma'am. I can deliver you home or wherever you would like to go."

Mercedes figured Raul must have called this man while she was on her way down to make sure she got home safely. Maybe he wasn't a complete ass.

Still ...

Smiling tightly, Mercedes allowed Lorenzo to escort her to the car. On her way home, she berated herself for the feeling of disappointment that washed over her. She once again reminded herself that she and Raul did not have a commitment, and she didn't even do commitments. Mercedes knew that type of relationship wasn't for her.

There was nothing to be disappointed about.

Yet, she couldn't explain the sense of longing that grew in the pit of her stomach the farther away from the hotel the car drove.

Farther away from Raul.

CHAPTER 1

Eighteen months later

Mercedes stood off to the side of the stage inside of the infamous Black Kitty. In front of her sat the short staircase that led up to the wooden stage, where she would be front and center for an audience of over a hundred and fifty patrons.

Her stomach fluttered with anticipation as she anxiously awaited the introduction for her to make her way onto the stage.

"Ladies and gentlemen, I know who you've all been waiting for," Mistress Coco, owner of The Black Kitty, began.

The audience cheered as Mistress Coco began her introduction.

"This next performer is hotter than a cat on a hot tin roof, Angelina Jolie's lips and Beyonce's ass put together!" Coco's naturally husky voice reverberated through the dimly lit room. "Give a warm welcome to the one, the *only*, Black Dahhhliiiaaa!"

Outfitted in her red and black Moulin Rouge costume, complete with a huge, feather tail, top hat, and cane, Mercedes strutted to the middle of the stage, pausing as the opening chords of Usher's "Bad Girl" began to play.

She smiled wickedly at the audience.

Tonight, Mercedes planned to take the audience on a ride.

Planting her cane and pivoting so her butt faced the crowd, Mercedes rotated her ass and swiveled her hips in time to the music, before turning and walking to the edge of the stage. She hooked one of the front male audience members with her cane and shook her breasts in his face before pushing him back into his seat.

The audience roared at her antics.

She took the cane in both hands in front of her, dipped down, spreading her legs wide, and gyrated her hips. Turning her back to the audience, she dropped the cane and removed her top hat, flinging it to the side of the stage. She knew that just out of view of the audience there was a stage kitten who would retrieve her costume items for her.

With a roll of her shoulders, she unbuttoned her corset, and spun, teasing the audience, showing one breast then the other, until she finally removed it, tossing it away. Same as she'd done with her hat. Mercedes dropped down to her knees and thrust her hips forward in a suggestive motion to the beat of the music. She raised herself on her forearms, her ass high in the air, and only her toes and forearms touching the floor.

She slowly dragged her toes forward, lifting her hips higher in the air, and rotated them in time with the beat. This was her signature move. It always got the crowd going, and tonight was no different.

The whistling, clapping, and stomping from the crowd got her adrenaline pumping even more. Mercedes dropped down, spun over so she was laying with her back on the stage, and bent her knees, lifting her hips and rotating in a circular motion and up and down in rhythm with the music.

Finally, she stood, turned her back to the crowd one last time, and removed the feather tail that was attached to her shorts with Velcro, exposing her barely-there panties. She finished her set in her stockings, purple pasties, and panties.

After bowing, she blew a kiss to the cheering audience before exiting the stage.

The rush she felt performing was like no other. In this space, Mercedes felt free of her concerns. She didn't worry about being assistant principal and the school year that was ending, her upcoming dreaded visit back home to see her family, or the strange hang up calls she had been getting.

Around The Black Kitty, Mercedes was just Black Dahlia, a smoking hot performer. Mercedes had had her share of lovers, many of whom were very good, and even they didn't compare to the pure, animalistic pleasure she derived from performing on stage.

The beat of the music, the adoration of the audience, and the support of the other dancers all touched a part of her spirit that nothing ever had before. On stage, Mercedes was unbidden by her family's conservative expectations, demands of her job, or societal expectation of how a "proper" woman was supposed to behave.

She was even thrilled to know her best friend, and fellow performer, Devyn Collins—who went by Black Pearl in the club—was in the audience cheering and supporting her.

Mercedes strolled down the long hallway adorned with new and old images of burlesque performers. She always felt a sense of pride seeing the images of women such as Josephine Baker, Jean Idelle, Lottie the Body, and others.

To be amongst the images of these groundbreaking women was an honor in the world of burlesque. Reaching the changing room, Mercedes entered and prepared to change as she waited for her costume. There was a knock on the door.

"Come in," Mercedes called.

A beat later, Roxxy, one of the stage kittens, entered, bringing Mercedes her discarded clothing.

"You were fantastic, Dahlia." Roxxy beamed at Mercedes.

Roxxy, like most of the stage kittens, was an up-and-coming performer, looking for a shot to perform one day on the big stage. She was fairly new to the club, but was as enthused as the other kittens to learn from the main performers.

"Thank you," Mercedes said, taking her costume from the younger woman.

"Maybe you can give me a few pointers some time?" Roxxy asked.

"Maybe, but it won't be for a while. I have a busy schedule over the next few months."

"Whenever you're—"

"Roxxy, come on, girl! These costumes aren't going to move themselves." Mistress Coco's voice blasted through the door.

Roxxy hesitated.

"You better go. Rule number one, *never* keep the boss lady waiting," Mercedes joked.

Owner of The Black Kitty, Mistress Coco was a five-foot-three powerhouse and former burlesque dancer herself. She was known to run a very tight ship when it came to her club. Even though the woman was in her mid-sixties, she was not someone whose bad side you wanted to get on.

"Yeah, I'll talk to you later," Roxxy said before rushing off.

Mercedes turned to look at herself in the mirror. She admired her strong, shapely legs, her flat stomach, and perky breasts. She examined her fishnet stockings, smokey eye makeup, and done up lips. This was how she felt most comfortable.

At times, she felt like the business suit professional was just a façade, but Black Dahlia was who she was meant to be all along. This made her think of the trip home she was scheduled to take in a few weeks. Her family knew nothing of this Mercedes.

She'd learned long ago that sharing all of who she was with her family was not acceptable.

* * *

RING. Ring. Ring.

"Dammit!" Mercedes cursed as she exited her bathroom.

It was the Sunday of Memorial Day weekend, around ten in the morning, and she was already running late. Today was not only Devyn and Nikola's Memorial Day picnic, but also the first birthday party for the couple's identical twins, Theodore and Jacques.

Mercedes had a few errands to run before making her way over to her friend's mansion, on the other side of town. If she was lucky, she'd make it there by noon, but this was Atlanta, and traffic was horrible.

Mercedes knew she wasn't going to be lucky today.

"Hello," Mercedes answered, picking up her apartment phone.

Silence.

"*Hello*," Mercedes said, a little more forcefully.

Silence.

A chill ran down Mercedes' spine. This was the third hang up call she had gotten that week. It was beginning to make her feel uneasy.

"Look, either you have something to say to me or not." Mercedes' anger was beginning to grow at the thought of someone intentionally trying to scare her.

Click.

Staring at the telephone receiver in her hand, Mercedes felt the tension grow in her stomach. She looked at the caller ID as she'd done with the previous hang up calls, and just like before, the number came up "Unknown".

Sighing, she hung the phone up, just before hearing the buzz of her cell phone. It was a text from Devyn.

Devyn: Hey, what time do you think you'll be here?

Mercedes paused before responding, thinking of the errands she needed to run, which included picking up the gifts she'd ordered for the boys.

Mercedes: Probably around 1 p.m. I woke up late and have to make a couple of stops first.

She waited a few minutes for Devyn's response.

Devyn: Alright. No problem. We'll see you then.

Mercedes: Hey, you didn't just try to call me on my home phone, did you?

Mercedes knew it was a long shot, but she hoped it was Devyn who called and hung up due to a bad connection or something.

Devyn: No. Why?

Mercedes: No reason. I'll see you later.

Once the conversation ended, Mercedes went to finish getting dressed. She styled her naturally kinky hair in a loose chignon and left a few curls hanging down the sides. She opted to wear a white chiffon, relaxed, long-sleeved dress. The slits extended the length of the sleeve, letting her feel comfortable wearing the dress in warm weather, while also allowing Mercedes to show off her toned arms. She matched the dress with a pair of three-inch, strappy sandals.

Checking the mirror once again, she looked over her light summer makeup, which usually consisted of a bit of concealer, some powder, eye shadow, and a bright lipstick. That day she opted to wear a shimmery pink color.

The bright colors against her dark skin made her skin glow even more.

Mercedes smiled, knowing she looked good.

Stepping out of her front door and walking to her car, Mercedes wondered if she would see Raul at the birthday party. For the past year and a half, she'd seen him only a handful of times. Mercedes knew from Devyn that he often traveled for work and to visit his family in Brazil.

The only times she'd seen him were when they both were christened as the twins' godparents, another time when Devyn and Nikola hosted a holiday party this past December, and a few times in passing when Raul and Mercedes had been visiting their friends' home.

She'd done her best to keep conversation to a minimum. At both the christening and the holiday party Raul had a different date on his arm. She knew he wasn't hurting for female attention.

Mercedes went out of her way to maintain her physical and emotional distance whenever he was around. Despite the emotional boundaries she tried to set she'd often find her eyes wandering and landing on his perfectly sculpted body. She couldn't help but notice the lingering stares he would send her way whenever they were in the same room.

The same combustible chemistry that pulled them together on the night of Devyn and Nikola's wedding was still there. Mercedes told herself it was simply because they'd never had the chance to finish what they started that night, but even after all this time she began to wonder if it wasn't something more.

Getting into her car, Mercedes closed her eyes to purge herself of thoughts of Raul Santiago. Instead, she found herself picturing a set of big, twinkling dark brown eyes.

She sighed.

Of course Raul will be there, he's the twins' godfather, she reminded herself.

Devyn still questioned Mercedes about what happened the night of her wedding with Raul, but she refused to tell her. She just admitted that things didn't work out between them and that was all. She knew Devyn didn't believe her, but she was not up for sharing any more details than necessary.

CHAPTER 2

Two hours later, Mercedes strolled up to her best friend's front door.

"Hey, gorgeous," Devyn greeted her as she pulled the door open.

Devyn and Nikola lived in a huge mansion in the exclusive community of Buckhead.

"Thank you. You're not looking too bad yourself, Mrs. Collins, mother of one-year-old twins." Mercedes eyed Devyn in her coral sleeveless romper, paired with white sandals. What made Devyn's look complete was the stunning smile and glow on her face.

"Thank you. How was the traffic?" Devyn asked as she pulled Mercedes into the house.

"Hell on Earth. You know how traffic is out here," Mercedes answered. She removed the bag holding the packages she had gotten for the boys from her shoulder. "Where do I put this?"

She'd gotten each twin a specialized baby book with all the pictures she'd taken over the last year, from the first day of their birth until now, and a number of specially made clothing items with their names embroidered on it, along with books and other smaller toys.

She loved spoiling her godsons.

"I told you not to go all out." Devyn tried to pin Mercedes with a serious look, but Mercedes waved her off.

"Girl, please. You know it's my job to spoil the hell out of my godchildren and then send them home to you and Nikola when they start crying."

She laughed when Devyn rolled her eyes.

"You're a pain in the butt," Devyn said, with her hands out. "I'll take those and put them with the rest of the gifts. You can head out back. Mostly everyone's already here."

Devyn took the gifts and walked toward the back of the house where there was a room for the children's gifts and toys.

Stepping outside into the backyard, Mercedes surveyed the entire scene in front of her. It was huge, with a custom-made outdoor grill, bar, and patio, on one end, and a large, in-ground swimming pool on the other end. Mercedes could see a number of Nikola and Devyn's family and friend's laying around or in the pool, while others sat at the tables that had been set up to accommodate the guests.

Not far from the grill she spotted Nikola holding one of the twins, while Raul held the other.

Mercedes was once again caught up in the sheer beauty of this man. No matter how many times she tried to remind herself that he was probably a no-good cheater, she couldn't help but stare.

Her lips began to tingle as memories of their explosive kisses danced in her mind.

He wore light-colored linen pants, and a light gray Polo shirt that was tucked in at the waist. The shirt's short sleeves showed off his rippling biceps. Mercedes bit her lip, as her eyes moved up to the big smile he wore while he tickled the chin of the twin he was holding. When the twin laughed, his smile was filled with almost as much pride as Nikola's.

Her heart rate sped up as she took in the picture he made before her.

One of pure masculinity and strength, but just enough vulnerability to play and laugh at the antics of the one-year-old child in his arms.

"Cute, aren't they?"

Mercedes jumped at hearing Devyn's voice behind her. "Dammit, girl, you know I've got high blood pressure. Why are you sneaking up on me like that?"

She tried to play off her surprise at once again being caught staring at Raul, but Devyn wasn't buying it.

"You have high blood pressure? Yeah right." Devyn laughed at Mercedes' incredulous face. "*Or* maybe you're just trying to play off getting caught once again staring at the godfather of my babies. One day you're going to tell me what went down between you two."

"Don't count on it," Mercedes mumbled, as Devyn pulled her over to say hello to Nikola, Raul, and the boys.

Mercedes greeted Nikola with a hug and placed a kiss on Theodore's cheek before turning to Raul.

"Mr. Santiago." Her greeting to Raul was shrouded in an icy stiffness.

Raul raised an eyebrow. "Killer, why must your friend insist on calling me Mr. Santiago?" Raul directed the question at Devyn but kept his attention on Mercedes.

Raul continued to call Devyn "Killer" ever since the night he and Nikola walked in on Devyn kicking the shit out of her ex-boyfriend. He'd jokingly offered her a job with his security firm, but Nikola quickly nixed that idea.

"I don't know, and since neither one of you will tell us what happened between you, I can only speculate," Devyn retorted, as she looked from Mercedes to Raul and back again.

"Well Santiago is your last name, isn't it?" Mercedes asked.

Raul sighed, before passing Jacques to Devyn since he began squirming for his mother.

"We'll let you two have a moment," Devyn said, eyeing Nikola, who'd silently been watching the exchange between their two best friends.

As Devyn and Nikola walked off with the boys, Raul allowed his gaze to slowly drift down Mercedes' body. She saw appreciation and a hint of lust in his eyes when they stopped on her pink-colored lips.

Her breath caught as she saw the look of lust grow, right before he blinked and it was gone.

"You're looking lovely, Mercedes. How have you been?" Raul asked.

"I'm great, *Mr. Santiago*." Mercedes made it a point to emphasize the last two words.

Just as Raul was about to respond, a blond-haired woman walked over. "Raul, sweetie, I'm getting hungry. Are you ready to eat?" she asked.

Mercedes found the woman's voice rather annoying. *And did she just call him sweetie?* Mercedes wondered if this was Cindy's replacement or if he had been so bold as to step out on Cindy with this woman. Raul didn't even bother to look ashamed of Mercedes seeing him with the woman he obviously came there with.

"Yvette, this is Mercedes. Devyn's best friend and godmother of the twins."

He had the nerve to introduce Mercedes to his date not thirty seconds after he'd just eyed her like she was a tall glass of water on a hot summer day.

Men.

Mercedes shook her head. After greeting Yvette, she excused herself to allow the couple some privacy. She spent the rest of the party playing with her godsons ... that was when the boys' grandmothers allowed them out of their sight long enough to play with someone else.

Mercedes secretly envied the way Devyn and Nikola's mothers gushed over their grandsons and their children in general. Both families had developed a special bond in the year and a half since their children married, and they would undoubtedly pass that closeness down to Theodore and Jacques.

Mercedes thought about her own family and felt a pang in her chest at the yearning for the closeness she saw in front of her. Not wanting to dwell on thoughts of her own family, Mercedes went over to ask Devyn about bringing the gifts out to let the boys open.

Fifteen minutes later, most of the guests gathered around the patio as Jacques and Theodore sat on their parents' laps, while ripping open their gifts. Mercedes laughed at the antics of the twins, who often seemed more interested in the wrapping paper than the actual gifts. It took nearly an hour to get through all of the presents that had been brought out.

More gifts remained in the boys' playroom, but Devyn opted to leave the rest until later. As Collins children, the twins had been born into a financial empire, and would want for nothing.

While the party began to wind down, Mercedes helped Devyn clean up the discarded wrapping paper, before heading out.

"You know if traffic is too crazy, you're more than welcome to stay the night," Devyn offered.

"I don't want to impose. I know your mom and the rest of your family are here," Mercedes countered.

Devyn waved her off. "Please, there's plenty of room."

"It's okay. I'll be all right getting home," Mercedes said, as they made their way through the house. She gave one last look at the boys.

"God, I can't believe they're a year already. Time flies," she said, with a hint of nostalgia in her voice.

"It sure does. I have toddlers already."

"Yeah, and I can't believe that's all you have with the way you and your husband go at it," Mercedes teased. She saw the loving kisses Nikola constantly snuck throughout the afternoon. She even noticed there was about a thirty-minute window, in which no one could find Nikola or Devyn.

Mercedes knew the two had probably snuck off to get busy.

"We don't have more kids yet because I perfected my swallowing technique."

Mercedes choked on the water she was drinking as she laughed at Devyn's statement.

"You're a trip. That husband of yours is rubbing off on you. I like it." Mercedes laughed again.

"Me too," Devyn said, as she hugged Mercedes.

"Leaving so soon?"

Devyn and Mercedes turned to see Raul approach.

"Yeah, I couldn't convince her to stay the night," Devyn answered.

"Uh, yeah. I've got some things I need to do tomorrow." Mercedes tightened her lips, wondering why she felt the need to explain herself to him.

"Let me walk you to your car," Raul offered.

Devyn's eyebrow rose, but she remained silent, as Raul grabbed Mercedes around the waist before she could protest.

Mercedes felt a sensation of warmth through her dress, where Raul's hand pressed into her lower back, as he opened the door, and Mercedes had to force herself not to lean into him.

"This wasn't necessary. I'm sure Yvette is wondering where you are," Mercedes said, in an attempt to remind herself, and him, that he was there with another woman.

Other than a small tick in his jaw, Raul continued leading toward her pine green Kia, without response. As they walked, Mercedes inhaled his scent. It was a mix of spice with a hint of sweetness. She hated the way the smell perfectly embodied him, and made her want to stick her nose in his neck and inhale even deeper.

"This is it. Thank you," she said as they arrived at her car. When she felt his hand still pressing on the small of her back, she turned to look up at him.

Raul nodded. "You're welcome, querida."

Mercedes didn't know what the last word meant, but she remembered he'd repeated it over and over when they kissed outside of his hotel room the night of the reception. She shivered just thinking of the way his lips felt as they moved over hers.

Her eyes dropped to his perfectly shaped lips as she licked her own. She didn't even notice until she saw Raul's lips turn up into a smile.

"See something you like?" he asked in that wicked tone that shot straight to her core.

"You wish," she said defiantly, pulling her gaze off his mouth and up to his eyes. And that was even worse because his eyes held a sinful gleam.

He knew she wanted him.

"I do," he said, his voice deepening.

Mercedes ignored the sudden tightening of her nipples.

"I don't think Yvette would appreciate you talking to me like this. And for that matter neither would Cindy. Or did you finally break up with her instead of just cheating on her?" Mercedes heard the anger in her own voice but didn't care.

However, Raul didn't rise to the bait. "I already told you I don't even know Cindy and I have not seen her since that night. As for Yvette, she's just a friend."

Mercedes eyed him closely. For some reason she believed him about Cindy, and maybe even Yvette. She couldn't blame the man for women coming onto him or being attracted to him. He was deliciously handsome, successful in his career, and very wealthy.

She looked into his eyes and knew that if given the chance he could make her fall hard for him.

She couldn't allow that.

"If you say so. But that's none of my damn business, anyway." She stepped back to unlock her car door.

"What if I wanted to make it your business?" he asked with a gleam in his eyes.

Mercedes tried hard not to smile, but the one he gave her was infectious.

She smiled as the butterflies in her stomach rose.

"I'm leaving now. Good-bye, Mr. Santiago." She used his last name in an attempt to assert some emotional distance.

"Raul," he stated in a low, but firm voice.

"What?" she asked, caught off guard.

"My name is Raul. Say it," he commanded.

"Mr. Sa—"

"Raul," he said more sternly, stepping closer to tower over her.

Mercedes felt the butterflies in her stomach turn into a full-on jackhammer as her insides hummed with desire under his watchful gaze. She wanted to be her usual defiant self and let him know she wasn't the least bit turned on.

But they both knew that would be a lie.

"Raul," she said, just above a whisper.

Those sexy lips of his once again turned up into a devil's grin. He'd won this round.

"That's more like it." He placed a kiss right at the corner of her lips. "Drive safely," he whispered in her ear before stepping back to allow her space to get into her car.

Then, he closed the door for her.

Driving off, Mercedes peeked at her rearview mirror to see Raul still standing in the center of the driveway watching her car. She couldn't help the smile that spread across her face.

CHAPTER 3

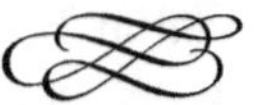

$\mathcal{R}$aul stood at the end of the driveway and watched Mercedes' car disappear around the corner. He didn't know why he felt the sense of longing grow the farther away she drove. Since the night of Devyn and Nikola's wedding, he'd wanted Mercedes. Bad.

To say he was pissed when he opened the door to find Cindy naked in his suite would be an understatement. He was truthful when he said he didn't know Cindy. She was actually a former fling of Nikola's. She had tried to sneak into the wedding reception with a date, but Raul personally escorted her out of the hotel, or so he thought.

Apparently, Cindy had other plans, and that night instead of leaving, she decided to turn her attention on him.

Raul later discovered that she bribed one of the hotel workers to find out what hotel suite he was staying in and to let her in. Unfortunately, Raul didn't find that out until after Mercedes stormed off. After he had Cindy escorted out, he went and found the assistant manager on duty. The same guy who fell for Cindy's bullshit.

Raul personally made sure the man was fired as a security specialist; he took that type of responsibility seriously. People's lives depended on security experts to do their damn jobs, and do it well. He knew more than anyone the type of damage that could be done by a crazed person with too much access to the object of their obsession.

Any manager allowing random women into a guest's hotel suite didn't deserve his job, as far as Raul was concerned.

Raul was never one to get caught up in a woman no matter how beautiful she was, and Raul was from Brazil. He knew beautiful women of all races and ethnicities. However, something about Mercedes drove him crazy. Not only was she beautiful, but she had a toughness that, for the most part, masked the vulnerability in her brown eyes.

On a sigh, Raul decided it was time for him to leave to take his date home. When he re-entered the house, he nearly bumped into Devyn who was still standing at the door, as if she'd never left. Her arms were folded and the expression on her face told him she wasn't playing.

"Hey, Killer. I was just about to grab Yvette and say my good-byes," he said.

"Mhm. What was that about?" she asked.

Raul knew exactly what she was referring to, but decided to play dumb. "What was what about?"

Devyn merely lifted her eyebrow, which made Raul smile. His best friend's wife was no pushover, and she was protective over her friend.

He blew out a breath. "I just wanted to make sure she got to her car safely. That's *all.*" He placed an emphasis on all despite the twisting in his gut that told him he was a damn liar.

By the expression on Devyn's face she knew it, too.

"Yeah, okay. Just know she's not only my friend, she's my sister, so if you hurt h—" Devyn raised her hand when Raul attempted to interrupt her. "*If* you hurt her, you'll have me to answer to. Got it?"

Raul smirked. "Are you going to sic that overgrown, half-Greek on me?" he joked, referring to Nikola.

"I'll do worse … I'll revoke your godfather privileges."

Raul frowned. She knew how much he loved his godsons.

"That's low, Killer."

"There you are. I was looking for you." They both turned to see Nikola entering the living room.

"Nik, tell your wife to stop threatening me," Raul told his friend.

"What's she doing? Warning you to not hurt Mercedes?" Nikola asked slyly.

"How'd you know?" Devyn's question held a hint of surprise.

Nikola shrugged. "She did the same when we first started dating," he said nonchalantly.

Devyn looked surprised to hear this. "No she didn't."

Nikola inclined his head. "She did. Not in so many words, but I got the message loud and clear." He chuckled.

Raul noted how much his friend laughed these days. It wasn't something he did often before dating Devyn. He saw the gleam of adoration in Nikola's eyes whenever he looked at his wife. If Raul had to admit it to himself, he wanted to experience the sort of love he saw between Devyn and Nikola.

An image of Mercedes popped into his mind.

"I'm going to go say my good-byes while you two make out or whatever," he said to the couple who'd quickly lost interest in him and were now engaged in their own little world. "See you both when I get back."

Raul was going to Rio to work with his father, and spend time with his mother, checking in on her. He looked forward to getting home to see them. Though it'd been years since anything occurred, Raul often made it a point to check-in on his parents in person to make sure they were okay.

He quickly shut the memories from his teenage years that caused his heart to skip a beat whenever he thought about how close he came to losing his mother out of his mind.

She's fine, he reminded himself as he went in search of the woman he'd brought to the party. It was time to head out.

CHAPTER 4

$\mathcal{M}$ercedes felt the burning in her chest as she ran along the neighborhood streets she grew up on.

It was her second full day visiting her parents, and she couldn't sleep past six o'clock. Instead of remaining in bed she decided to go out for a run. Mercedes' parents lived in the Houston suburb of Pearland. As she ran, Mercedes reminisced on growing up in this community.

Her chest tightened as she ran past the church where her father had been a preacher for over forty years. She'd spent many days in that brick building with the large, wooden cross on the top. To her it looked more like a prison than a place of worship.

A woman's place is in the home tending to her family.

Mercedes remembered the words her father often repeated from the pulpit and to her throughout her childhood.

Shaking her head to rid herself of the memory, she slowed her gait from a run to a light jog, and then a walk to cool down before stretching. Mercedes snorted as she held onto the metal fence that surrounded her parents' home. The chastisements of her father mingled with the childhood images she had of her father leaving right after dinner and not returning until late at night, or even sometimes the following morning.

She often asked her mother why he left so frequently, and her mother responded that he was helping members of the church who were going through difficult times. But Mercedes thought about the way her mother would wince whenever Mercedes asked this question. Or the way her mother's chin trembled as she forced a smile on her face, as she told Mercedes the lie.

Even as a child, Mercedes knew her father wasn't simply taking care of church business.

More than a few times, while doing laundry, Mercedes saw lipstick stains on the collar of her father's shirts. Her mother never wore lipstick.

"How was your run?"

Mercedes turned to see her mother peering out of the front door. At fifty-three, Mercedes' mother's mahogany skin remained smooth, and although she'd gained weight since Mercedes was a child, she still looked good. Even though her wardrobe was a little on the dull side.

Linda had her relaxed hair pulled back in a bun, which was how she most often wore it. She was wearing a pair of black slacks and a gray T-shirt that was covered by an apron, to prevent stains from the big brunch she'd gotten up early to prepare.

Mercedes couldn't help but think of Devyn before she'd broken up with that asshole of an ex of hers. Her friend often wore dowdy clothing that hid her curves and failed to compliment her complexion. Mercedes' mother's wardrobe over the last thirty years was akin to Devyn's old, bland style.

Mercedes' mother taught her it was the duty of a wife to always wake up before her husband. It was not ladylike to sleep longer than the man of the house. Mercedes nearly rolled her eyes at that thought, since she knew her father had once again been out late the night before.

"It was good, Mama. Hey, do you know what I was thinking?" Mercedes asked her mother as she moved around the fence into the yard.

"What's that, sweetie?" Linda Holmes squinted as she looked on curiously.

Not for the first time, Mercedes saw how beautiful her mother was. She had flawless skin and her kindness shone through.

"What if the two of us went shopping later on today? I need to pick up some new clothes for …" Mercedes trailed off, stopping just in time before she blurted out that needed items for a new burlesque set she was planning.

Her family didn't know about her dancing.

"I saw there's a new makeup store in town. We could go check it out and get our makeup done," Mercedes suggested.

"Oh," Linda tutted, waving her hands as if shooing Mercedes away. "An old lady like me wearing makeup?" She laughed.

A pang of sadness hit Mercedes' belly. She couldn't help but compare her mother to Mistress Coco. The owner of The Black Kitty was probably ten years older than her mother but lived life like she was in her twenties or thirties. Mercedes wanted some of that energy for her mother.

"You're not old," Mercedes insisted. "And you would look stunning with a little blush and maybe some eyelash extensions."

Linda sucked her teeth. "I am not putting those caterpillar looking things on my eyelids."

Mercedes let out a laugh. "Okay, that might be a bit too much for you right now. But how about a new tint with some colored lip gloss and maybe a nice eye shadow?"

Her mother gave her a wary look.

"Please, Mama? It doesn't have to be anything too much." The main reason Mercedes made these annual trips back home was to spend time with her mother, and her brother.

Jamal would be over later for breakfast, and Mercedes already made plans to spend a few nights at her brother's place to catch up with him. She really wanted to take the day to connect with her mother.

A small smile edged its way across Linda's lips. "I guess we can do that. But not until after we've all had breakfast, and that's if your father doesn't have anything planned for the family."

Mercedes just barely kept her eye roll to herself. Her father was the last person she wanted to spend the day with.

"Okay. Do you need any help in the kitchen?" she asked as she followed her mother into the house.

"No, you gon' ahead and shower and get dressed. Mal will be here around ten to have breakfast with us," Linda said, referencing Mercedes' younger brother, Jamal.

Mercedes placed a kiss on her mother's cheek before heading up to her childhood room to shower and change. Mercedes attempted to mentally fortify herself for the onslaught of questions she knew were coming during their meal.

"Hey! Hey! Hey! Big sis. What's up, girl?" Jamal's deep, boisterous voice rang through the house as he entered the door a few hours later. Four years her junior, Jamal was one of Mercedes' favorite people in the world.

She smiled widely and ran to hug her brother. "Mal! It's about time you showed up. I was about to make a trip to the nearest fast food place. You know Mama wouldn't let us eat without you and I'm starving." Mercedes laughed.

"Nah, you can't start without me. I'm not that late."

Mercedes glowered at the six-foot, former high school linebacker. Jamal was a few shades lighter than Mercedes, with a warm chestnut hue, strong, chiseled jaw, and big, brown eyes that were always inviting.

At Mercedes' gaze, Jamal dipped his head and ran a hand along the back of his neck. He was thirty minutes late. Mercedes laughed at his expression, rarely ever able to remain mad at her little brother.

A few minutes later their father came downstairs, and their mother began placing the food on the table that Mercedes had already set. Dwayne Holmes stood at five feet ten inches, with smooth skin that extended all the way to his bald head that he shaved regularly.

They hadn't been allowed to eat until the man of the house took his seat first. That was one of the rules in her parents' home.

Once Dwayne took his seat, Mercedes' mother immediately placed a full plate in front of him. Mercedes watched as her father planted his elbows on the table and swept his gaze over the food and placements before finally looking over at her.

Mercedes held in a breath as she anticipated what the next words out of her father's mouth would be.

"Mercedes, are you seeing anyone?" he asked before he began cutting into the slice of ham on his plate.

Mercedes placed her white cloth napkin in her lap and waited for her brother to pass her the plate of eggs. "No, sir. I am not currently seeing anyone."

"Mmmm." He nodded. "Well, you know no man wants a woman too far over thirty to settle down with. Nor does he want a woman who's been around the block with too many men."

Mercedes bit back her reply, choosing instead to bite into one of her mother's homemade biscuits.

"Dad, can you pass me the orange juice please?" Jamal interrupted when Dwayne opened his mouth to say something else.

"Sure, son."

Like night and day.

Dwayne Holmes treated his baby boy like a prince, while he often treated Mercedes like a burden, especially after she left for college. Dwayne believed Mercedes going off to college in Washington DC was a direct betrayal to all he taught her growing up.

He doesn't know the half of it, Mercedes thought to herself, realizing if her father knew about her life in Atlanta, he'd have a fit.

Dwayne Holmes would blow a gasket if he found out that Mercedes was a burlesque performer, let alone the fact that she had a history of dating men and women.

"Like I was saying, no man is going to want a woman who's been around the block. A wife of …"

Noble character is her husband's crown, but a disgraceful wife is like decay in his bones. Mercedes completed the Bible verse in her head that her father drilled into her as a child.

She forked eggs into her mouth to keep her mouth occupied instead of firing back at her father.

Fuck. It's going to be a long week, Mercedes thought as she chewed and swallowed her eggs.

"Yes, Dad," she said with what she hoped looked like a believable smile on her face.

"Dad, how about you tell us about the next sermon you have planned?" Jamal asked.

Mercedes glanced over at her brother and gave him an appreciative smile.

Their father spent the next fifteen minutes telling them about the sermon he had planned for the following week. Ironically, it was on the teachings of fidelity. Mercedes could almost laugh at the ridiculousness, if it wasn't so sad.

CHAPTER 5

As soon as Raul stepped across the threshold into his childhood home a sense of ease fell over him. He inhaled the fresh smell of lemons that he knew was from the cleaning solution his mother always used.

His parents' spacious, four-bedroom, three-bathroom house, with panoramic views of a lagoon was located in the exclusive Lagoa Rodrigo de Frietas community in Rio.

Raul closed the door behind him and immediately checked the touchpad of the security system mounted on the wall next to the door.

"Filho! It's about time you've come home," Raul's mother greeted just as he turned from ensuring the alarm was on and functioning. Since it was just him, he'd never felt the need to buy a home when he came to Rio. He was close with his parents and knew they missed him when he was away, so he preferred to stay with them when he visited.

"Alo, Mama! I missed you, too," he greeted his mother as she placed kisses on his cheeks.

"Manny, vem aqui!" his mother yelled for his father. At five foot three and barely reaching his shoulder in her heels, his mother was a petite ball of energy. Rosaline Santiago was a beautiful woman whose light, creamy skin, hazel eyes, and long, curly hair spoke to her mixed Portuguese and native Brazilian ancestry.

Raul felt a shift in his chest as he stared at his smiling mother. Though he knew she was good, it always gave him a small sense of relief to lay his eyes on her and see that she was doing well.

There had been many years when he was younger that he'd watched his mother try to hide her hallowed eyes that filled with fear at the sound of any little thing. His mother had had a stalker for years, which nearly ruined their entire family.

"Filho!" Raul heard his father's deep voice as he entered the room.

At six foot two, the same golden complexion as his son, and salt and pepper hair, Raul's father was an exact replica of what Raul would look like in another thirty years. Manuel Santiago was the founder and current CEO of one of the oldest and most successful banks in Brazil, Banco Rio.

Raul came home throughout the year, in part to work with his father in the home office. He also did a lot of the security for his father's bank, ensuring that their systems were updated.

With Raul's background having attended military college, proceeded by fulfilling his military obligations in the U.S. Army, and then creating his own private security firm, Raul's father trusted his son more than anyone to assist with the bank's security.

Not to mention, Manuel knew where Raul's drive to protect his family came from. He also understood that Raul's experience of seeing his mother stalked when he was younger gave him the desire to fiercely protect the ones he loved most.

"Alo, Papa," he greeted his father with a kiss on each cheek.

"Are you hungry, filho?" his mother asked.

He'd eaten a little on the plane, but wanted to save room for his mother's cooking. She loved making a big, traditional Brazilian meal whenever he returned.

He smiled knowingly. "Estou com fome, Mama." He responded in the affirmative knowing she loved nothing more than feeding her only son.

His father grunted.

"Every day she's telling me to eat more fruits and vegetables. Stop eating too much meat. Drink more water. You come home and she's in the kitchen cooking up a four-course meal," Raul's father teased, shaking his head.

Raul knew his mother often chided his father on his eating habits, and she was known to pop in at his office at lunch time to make sure he ate the healthy meals she prepared for him instead of something else.

Raul spent the rest of the afternoon and evening eating the meal his mother prepared and catching up with his parents. Over the years, they'd become more like close friends, instead of just child and parents.

Raul's mother often questioned him for not being married yet, asking when she was going to get to be a grandmother. He knew it came from a place of love, so he didn't mind it … except when she partnered with his second mother, Iris Collins.

The two women together could be like a dog with a bone. Relentless.

Tired, Raul stood, taking his suitcases to his room, and unpacked, looking forward to spending the next few weeks with his family.

* * *

OVER THE COURSE of the next three weeks, Raul spent his days between the bank with his father, and also double and triple checking the security system of his parents' home.

"You know you don't have to do that, right?" Raul's mother said in her native Portuguese as she came up behind him in their backyard.

Raul had been checking the cameras that were mounted on the sides of the house. He wanted to make sure there wasn't anything obstructing their view.

He turned to her. "I needed to check before I leave tomorrow." His time in Brazil had flown by.

His mother shook her head and gave him a small grin. "What you need to do is find you a wife so you can make me a grandmother."

Raul peered up at the brilliant blue sky, his arms dropping to his sides as if he was exhausted. His mother chuckled as she came to a stop in front of him.

"I'm serious, filho. Stop worrying about all of this security stuff and find yourself a wife."

"Mama," he murmured.

"Don't Mama me. You've been single long enough. Even Nikola has settled down."

Fucking Nikola. Ever since his friend married and started a family, Raul's mother had been relentless in getting Raul to do the same.

"In time, Mama," Raul said, trying to appease her.

Rosaline shook her head. "You keep saying that. How much time does it take to find a beautiful woman to settle down with? Nikola found his Devyn at work. Maybe you should hire some more women at your security firm," she suggested.

Raul laughed. "Hiring a woman solely for the chance to date her is called sexual harassment."

"Blah." His mother folded her arms across her chest and gave him a look. Raul did his best not to squirm underneath her gaze. The look in her eyes turned serious. "I know why you hold back from dating. You think what happened to me will happen to your future wife."

Raul shook his head, wanting this conversation to end, but Rosaline continued.

"You know what happened to me … that man …" She paused, her eyes hitting the grass beneath their feet before she peered back up at her son. "He was sick Raul."

Raul tightened his fists at his sides, hating this topic. He knew the man who'd met his mother one day at a grocery store in town and ended up stalking her for years was sick. But in the years since, he'd worked too many cases of people who were *sick* committing unspeakable acts against those they were obsessed with.

He knew his mother had gotten off lucky. And yes, he would admit, it made him hesitant when it came to the thought of a long-term relationship.

Rosaline placed a hand on Raul's wrist, squeezing it gently. "You deserve to find someone who you can be happy with. Like your father and me."

Raul simply nodded, his throat too constricted to speak.

Thankfully, his mother let the conversation die there. He went on to finish his tasks of making sure the property's security system was in good working order, before heading up to his bedroom to take a shower. The second floor of the house was considered Raul's space.

The entire time he showered, he thought about the brief conversation he had with his mother. Raul hated that the traumatic history still seemed to cast a shadow over his life. His mother was no longer the frightful woman who never left the house. Regardless, Raul would never forget the tormented look in her eyes whenever the phone rang or there was a knock on the door.

He recalled the way his father would peer out the windows anytime a car passed or unlock and relock the household windows and doors every night just to make sure the house was secure.

Those memories don't fade easily. Especially not with his line of work.

As Raul wrapped a towel around his waist and took a seat on the edge of his bed, his cell phone rang.

He answered even though he didn't recognize the number. "Hello."

"Hi, Raul. It's Mercedes." Raul was surprised but not unhappy to hear Mercedes' voice on the other end of the phone.

"Querida." His voice was smooth as silk as he acknowledged her with his favorite term of endearment for her.

"I hope I'm not bothering you. I got your number from Devyn a while back, in case of emergencies and things like that, not to like … Never mind. I was just trying to get in touch with Devyn and haven't been able to. I wanted to know if you'd spoken to or seen her or Nikola recently?" she asked.

Her voice sent shivers down his spine, and he closed his eyes, picturing her beautiful face.

Sitting on the side of his large bed, he responded, "No. I've been in Brazil the last few weeks working and visiting family."

"Oh shit, I didn't mean to bother you while you're with your family," she apologized.

"It's fine. You're not interrupting," he told her, thinking she would hang up before he really got a chance to talk with her. "Was there something wrong? I mean, why did you need Devyn?" He figured she must need something important if she was calling him to locate Devyn.

"No, nothing's wrong. I'm flying back to Atlanta tomorrow from Houston, and Devyn is supposed to pick me up from the airport. I wanted to tell her I caught an earlier flight."

Raul did know from Devyn that Mercedes grew up around Houston.

"Ah, so you're visiting family also?" He leaned back on his headboard with one hand propped behind his head.

"Yup." Mercedes' voice was clipped as if she didn't want to talk about her family, but that was too damn bad since she'd called him.

The urge to know more about Mercedes overtook him.

"How is Houston this time of year?" he asked, trying to ease into the conversation.

"Hot." She laughed.

He felt his chest tighten with an unfamiliar feeling at hearing her breathy laugh. "Do you have any siblings?"

"You're nosy, aren't you? Why don't you tell me about *your* family," she said, turning the tables on Raul.

He had no problem talking about his family. Over the next ten minutes Raul told Mercedes the story of his parents meeting in college in New York City, falling in love, and then moving back home to Brazil.

"Wow, your father started an actual bank?" she asked, sounding intrigued.

"He did," Raul responded with pride. "I do some work for the bank which is why I come home from time to time."

Mercedes listened intently, asking questions here and there, while revealing a few details about her own family. It wasn't lost on Raul that he did most of the sharing. He wondered what it was about her background that Mercedes didn't want to reveal. Just as he was going to pry, Mercedes' other line beeped.

"Hey, that's Devyn. I gotta go."

Raul hated to let her go. For a short while, she'd let down her guard. Their conversation was brief but easy. He instantly craved more of it. Just as he'd craved more of her the night of Nikola and Devyn's wedding.

But as with that night, their time together was too brief. Oddly, his mother's harassing him about needing to settle down penetrated his mind. He shook her voice out of his head, but he couldn't shake his desire to get to know more about Mercedes.

He'd already been intrigued by Mercedes, and their short phone conversation served to pique his interest even more. Raul could tell she was skittish when it came to getting to know him, but in that moment, he decided she would have to get over that.

Raul always went after what he wanted and what he wanted was Mercedes.

CHAPTER 6

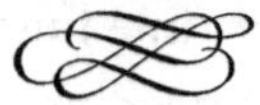

ercedes watched as Devyn's dark gray BMW SUV pulled up to the sidewalk at Atlanta International Airport the following afternoon.

"Hey, girl!" Devyn greeted. She hopped out of the car and hugged Mercedes before they loaded her bags into the trunk compartment since the backseat was filled with Devyn's twins and their car seats. Mercedes leaned in and placed kisses on each of her godsons' cheeks, and then got into the passenger seat.

"How was your trip?" Devyn asked as she pulled off.

She sighed dramatically. "Ugh, long."

"That bad, huh?"

"Worse."

Mercedes told Devyn all about her trip, including her father's jabs about her life, as they drove to lunch at a popular restaurant. Even though it was the middle of the lunch rush, the restaurant accommodated the two women with a private room, which was good for the boys to move around without disturbing other patrons.

"How's Jamal?" Devyn asked as she wiped Theodore's face.

"Still pissed you got married."

Devyn laughed.

Mercedes' brother had had a long-term crush on Devyn.

"Oh, please." Devyn waved Mercedes off. "You know he's got plenty of women to keep him company."

They both laughed.

Mercedes' younger brother was a bit of a playboy in his own right.

They spent the next hour eating and catching up. Mercedes told Devyn all about her upcoming travel plans for the summer, which included burlesque tours while school was on break.

This summer she had scheduled performances in New York, Chicago, and New Orleans, in addition to her regular performances at The Black Kitty and some smaller venues in a few other cities in Georgia.

After finishing their meal, they gathered the boys, went back to the car, and then headed toward Mercedes' home.

"I bought a few things for my costumes while I was there. Oh, and I even got my mom to go shopping with me. I had to tell her that I was buying a feather boa for a school play I'm putting on next school year." Mercedes chuckled at the lie she'd given her mother when asked about the extravagant costume items she'd purchased on their shopping trip.

"You could just tell your family the truth," Devyn said, giving her a look out of the corner of her eye before peering back at the road.

"Yeah right." Mercedes clucked her tongue. "My father would have a freaking aneurysm, and my mother would likely die of embarrassment." She didn't like lying to her parents ... well, not her mother. Mercedes always wanted a closer relationship with her mother, but her father's old school beliefs and the fact that he was a huge hypocrite kept her from being honest with them.

"I called Raul yesterday looking for you," Mercedes said to change the subject, then wanted to slap her forehead for bringing up Raul.

Now Devyn was staring at her with a raised eyebrow.

"What? What the hell is that look for?" Mercedes asked defensively.

"Watch your mouth," Devyn said, referring to the twins. "I'm just curious. What's going on with you two?"

Mercedes shrugged. "Nothing's going on with us. I don't even trust him."

Devyn frowned. "Why not? Did he do something to you?" she asked cautiously.

"No, nothing like that. I mean …" Mercedes finally told Devyn what transpired between Raul and her the night of the wedding. Mercedes could feel her anger and embarrassment rise as she told the story.

When she was finally done talking, she expected Devyn to look just as shocked or even angry as she was, but she was surprised.

Instead of being angry, Devyn began laughing.

"What the fu— heck are you laughing at?" she asked, irritated that Devyn would laugh at her.

Devyn waved her hand. "It's not you I'm laughing at. Well … maybe. Girl, Raul wasn't dating Cindy. She's not Raul's ex. Actually, she's Nikola's."

Mercedes raised an eyebrow. "Nikola's?"

"Mhm." Devyn nodded, as she proceeded to tell Mercedes about Cindy and how she tried to sneak into the wedding reception, and that it was Raul's security team who kicked her out.

"She probably decided to turn her sights on Raul seeing as how Nikola was no longer available."

"Dada!" Jacques yelled out at hearing his father's name mentioned.

Both women laughed.

"Anyway, I know for a fact there was never anything going on between Raul and Cindy. He would never date a woman that Nikola dated."

Mercedes thought about everything Devyn had revealed. For the last year and a half, she'd thought of Raul as a two-timing bastard like her father. Maybe it was her fear of falling for a man who was like her father that really caused her to put up a wall between her and Raul.

Just thinking about him brought up emotions Mercedes was not ready to deal with, and she wasn't sure if she would ever be.

To say she had trust issues was an understatement. They spent the rest of the ride in silence, except for the babbling of the boys.

Devyn pulled into the parking lot of Mercedes' apartment complex. Mercedes had a two-bedroom, outfacing apartment that was located on the second floor of her building. They each carried a twin, and one of Mercedes' bags. Mercedes loved her apartment and coming home to it felt like a respite after spending the last few days with her parents.

She wanted to sigh with relief as she opened the door, but comfort was the last emotion she felt as she laid eyes on her apartment.

Mercedes' breathing stalled. She flicked on the light and gasped at the destruction before her.

"Wha—" Devyn gasped as she took in the damage to Mercedes' apartment.

All her belongings were thrown on the floor, her leather couches were shredded as if someone took a pair of scissors to them, and her television had been ripped from the wall and smashed onto the floor.

As if all that wasn't bad enough, the word "BITCH" was smeared in big, red letters on the living room wall.

Blinking away tears at the destruction of all her belongings, Mercedes took a step to inspect the rest of her apartment, but Devyn's hand stopped her.

"No, you can't go any farther," Devyn insisted. "Let's step outside and call the police. Whoever did this may still be inside." Devyn pulled out her cell phone to dial 911.

Mercedes knew Devyn was right, but she had to see the extent of the destruction. She wondered who would do something like this to her. Was it a random act or was this someone she knew?

She began taking another step, but Devyn grabbed her arm again.

"No. You're not going in there, especially as long as you have my son in your arms," she reiterated worriedly.

Mercedes peered down at Theodore who looked curiously around the room. Devyn was right, she didn't know what the rest of her apartment was like, and she didn't want her godson to witness anymore horror.

She relented and stepped back toward the door on shaky legs. Mercedes' body trembled with fear and rage as they waited outside of her apartment for the police, Devyn stroking her arm reassuringly. She was glad to have her friend with her at that moment. She didn't know how she would have reacted coming home and seeing her apartment destroyed if she were by herself.

About ten minutes later the police showed up to take her statement and go with her as she inspected the rest of her apartment. When she entered her bedroom, her heart plummeted. Out of all her belongings, her burlesque costumes were what she was most proud of.

Most of her costumes she'd made herself, by hand. She spent hours sewing garments together or gluing rhinestones to her corsets. She wanted to be in control of every aspect of her performance, which included her look.

All of her work had been destroyed.

Her costumes lay in tatters on her bedroom floor. She couldn't stop the tears that rolled down her cheeks. Sniffing, she gave the officers her statement and told them all the damage she saw that had been done. She didn't see that anything was stolen, just destroyed.

Devyn came in with the boys in her arms and told Mercedes she would stay with her and Nikola until she felt it was safe to return. Mercedes thanked the officers, and called her landlord. They waited while an employee from her office apartment came to record all the damage that had been done.

The police discovered the lock on Mercedes door had been tampered with, so the employee put in to have the locks changed. Mercedes was grateful for the items of clothing she'd had with her while in Houston. It looked like whoever did this trashed the rest of her clothes, too.

Devyn hugged Mercedes as they stood by her car. "We can stop by the store and pick up some things on the way to my place."

Mercedes just nodded before climbing into the passenger seat. She knew she was too shaky to drive at the moment. She would come back in the next day or two to pick up her car.

Mercedes was in a daze as they picked up clothing items for her at the store. The same questions kept popping into her head over and over.

Had this been a random act? If not, who would have so much hate for her? Could it be one of her exes?

She tried to think of all the people she'd dated over the last few years. None stuck out as ending particularly badly, but she knew, from growing up with her father, how some people presented the outside world one image, meanwhile they hid their true colors behind closed doors.

Even as Mercedes thought of these questions, she knew this wasn't a random act. Mercedes began to realize whoever had done this was likely behind the hang up calls she'd been having.

The dread and anxiety in the pit of her stomach began to increase the more she thought about it.

Mercedes started to feel something she'd rarely felt since moving out of her parents' home. Real fear.

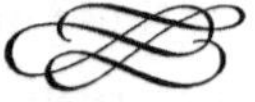

CHAPTER 7

*R*aul slid his dark Cartier sunglasses up the brim of his nose as he got behind the wheel of his Porsche Cayenne. The phone call he'd gotten the night before from Nikola caused him to change his plans for the day. As soon as he heard the tension in his friend's voice, he knew something was wrong.

Nikola did not get agitated easily, but learning that his wife and sons were with Mercedes when they found her apartment broken into and in disarray had Nikola on edge.

For his part, Raul's heart rate sped up at the knowledge that Mercedes was in danger. Raul's firm specialized in family security, and he came across a number of stalking cases. When Nikola described the damage that had been done to Mercedes' apartment his stomach dropped.

If this was what he believed it was, Mercedes was in real danger.

The thought of Mercedes' safety being jeopardized bothered him more than he cared to admit to anyone but himself. The first stop he planned to make was to Mercedes' apartment.

He would be able to get a look at the damage for himself and assess the situation.

Raul entered Mercedes' apartment with the key the woman at the front office had given him. The fact that he was able to flash his famously charming smile and make a little small talk to convince the woman to turn over a key to the apartment was not a good sign.

He'd merely told her he was a friend picking up some clothing and the woman was all too happy to do his bidding.

If Mercedes returned to her apartment, he would definitely need to speak with management. Entering the apartment, Raul was struck by the sheer destruction. Raul stepped over the scattered and torn books that laid all over the floor, looked over the cut-up leather couches, and saw the smashed television.

His eyes narrowed as he paused in front of the spray-painted curse on the wall.

His footsteps were barely audible as he made his way down the hall, letting his gaze take in every inch of the destruction. In the bedroom he was met with just as much of a mess. The mattress was slashed. Raul stopped short when something crunched beneath the weight of his foot.

Moving back, he noted the tiny beads and sequins scattered all over the floor by the closet. Inside of the closet, he saw more shredded clothing, feathers strewn around, and rhinestones, beads, and sequins tossed about. The closet was a particular mess with more vile curses spray painted on the inside.

Raul knew Mercedes danced burlesque though he'd never seen her perform. From the closet, he could tell performing was something Mercedes was very proud of, and whoever had destroyed her apartment knew that.

Whoever the person was, they wanted to cause Mercedes emotional pain, distress, and most of all fear.

Raul's protective instincts kicked into high gear as he looked over Mercedes' apartment one last time. He knew the person responsible for the warzone before him wouldn't stop at destroying Mercedes' belongings.

Raul's hands tightened into fists at his sides. A wash of anger overcame him. He closed his eyes and a picture of a smiling Mercedes appeared behind his eyelids. He didn't know who the hell was behind this mess, but he wouldn't let the bastard get away with it. And he damned sure wouldn't let this person harm one hair on Mercedes' head.

From here on out, whoever this was would have to go through him to get to her, and even the most determined stalkers hadn't gotten through him.

* * *

WHEN RAUL ARRIVED at Nikola and Devyn's, he was let in by the housekeeper. She escorted him to the back patio where Nikola, Devyn, Mercedes, and the boys were eating lunch. On the way over he'd called his top security expert to begin their investigation, which would begin with his employee asking questions of Mercedes' neighbors and apartment office.

However, Raul needed to speak with Mercedes to begin compiling a list of suspects. He also had a feeling she would balk at the security plan he'd come up with, but she would just have to deal with it.

"Why in the fu—"

Raul watched as Devyn shushed Mercedes to stop the curse word from coming out.

"Heck would you involve him?" Mercedes asked, incredulously.

Raul had an inkling that he was the *him* she referred to. Mercedes' back was to him, so she hadn't seen him enter. He purposely remained still to not alert her of his presence. Nikola saw Raul, but Raul shook his head, silently telling Nikola not to give his presence away.

Years serving together and as best friends gave the men the ability to communicate with one another without exchanging a single word.

"Because someone obviously means to do you harm and Raul can help," Devyn defended.

"How do we even know this wasn't a random act? Whoever this was could have just seen I wasn't there for a few days and wanted to cause damage for whatever reason."

Raul had thought about the possibility that the break-in could be an arbitrary act of destruction. Unfortunately, as soon as he saw the vandalization of Mercedes' apartment, he knew that wasn't the case.

It was no random act.

He knew with every fiber of his being that Mercedes was the intended target. And what Devyn said next only confirmed this for him.

"Mercedes, it's doubtful this was some stranger with nothing better to do," Devyn replied. "You told me last night you've been getting hang up calls for weeks now. I still can't believe you're just now telling me. Those calls and your apartment break-in are not just a coincidence."

Raul watched as Devyn leveled a serious look at her friend. Her eyes were filled with concern and fear. He knew that look, and he agreed with her.

Nikola hadn't told him about the hang up calls the night before, but Raul tucked this new information away to investigate later. Whoever was behind those calls decided to elevate their level of intimidation and struck Mercedes' apartment while she was away.

"Okay, you're probably right about that, but do you think it was necessary to have to get Raul involved? I'm sure we can let the police handle it," Mercedes conceded. "Isn't he still in Brazil anyway?"

At that, Raul decided it was time to intervene in the conversation.

"The police are already involved," Raul stated casually, as he sauntered out onto the patio.

Both women seemed surprised to see him. Raul didn't miss the look of appreciation Mercedes gave him as her gaze perused up and down his tall frame. But as soon as her eyes met his, she blinked, masking her expression.

"And no, I'm no longer in Brazil." He tossed her a grin. "Thanks for thinking of me, though."

Devyn stood and walked to greet him. "Raul."

He then patted Nikola's shoulder before placing a kiss on each of his sleeping godsons' heads. Mercedes eyed him suspiciously as he took a seat nearby.

"I hope you didn't cut your trip short on my account." She tried to come across as nonchalant, but he saw something deeper. A look of fear that told him that inside she was feeling the opposite of the casual image she tried to portray.

"I spent enough time in Brazil."

"I just mean this probably isn't a big deal," Mercedes said quickly.

"Oh, really?" he questioned.

"Yes, I mean maybe both the hang up calls and break-in are related and maybe not. What if whoever did this targeted a random apartment and it happened to be mine? Those sorts of things happen all of the time." She shrugged. "It sucks, but it happens."

Raul leaned back in his chair and stared at Mercedes as she began tapping the table with her finger. It was a nervous tick he'd seen many times before from clients. Often, it wasn't people's words, but the subconscious acts they weren't aware of that gave them away.

Mercedes didn't even believe the words she was saying, but she was struggling to make sense of being the target of an obviously off-balanced individual.

"You're right. Random acts of violence happen all the time. This could very well be the case for you …" He paused.

Mercedes sat a little taller in her chair, a satisfied smirk appearing on her face.

"But it's not," he said sternly.

The look of relief in her eyes quickly faded. "How do you know that?"

Raul held his hand up. "I know because I've worked on more than fifty stalking cases. I know the different types of stalkers, their motives, and their intent. The person targeting you is the most dangerous type of stalker."

Raul withheld that his very first experience with stalking was when he was just a teenager. Unfortunately, he was very familiar with these types of obsessions.

He paused to let what he said sink in. His goal wasn't to scare Mercedes, but he needed to make her understand the severity of the situation. This wasn't some kid who was out to trash the first empty apartment they found.

"I have years of experience dealing with these types of stalkers, and I've been to your apartment. Whoever this is, is targeting *you*. They are angry as hell at *you* for whatever reason. My job is to figure out who it is before their behavior escalates."

Raul watched as the awareness and fear rose in Mercedes' eyes. His heart squeezed at seeing the usually confident, self-assured woman in front of him come to grips with the fact she was the victim of a stalker.

"Raul—" Devyn went to speak, but Nikola's hand on her arm interrupted her.

"I think we should let Raul and Mercedes speak in private," Nikola stated.

Devyn eyed her husband, not wanting to leave her friend, but Nikola was adamant.

"Let's put the boys in their cribs while Raul and Mercedes talk." He rose and moved to pull out Devyn's chair.

Devyn finally relented and went around the table, placing a reassuring arm on Mercedes' shoulder, before picking up Theodore and heading into the house with Nikola carrying Jacques.

Raul turned his attention fully to Mercedes. She still looked as if she was processing what he just told her. The finger that had been tapping the hardwood table before was still, but Raul could see that her leg continued to bounce ... another telltale sign.

"Mercedes ..." He trailed off as her gaze met his.

"No," she said, lifting her hand in the air. "How do you know? How can you be sure?"

She was still trying to fight the obvious. It was a defense mechanism that Raul was familiar with.

He stood and moved to the chair next to her.

"Look at me," he demanded.

As she turned her body to face him, he grasped both of her hands in his. He felt the slight tremor in her hand and cursed himself for being the one to have to deliver such news to her.

Still, he had to make her understand the threat she faced. His heart squeezed again as she lifted her big brown eyes to his and he saw the fear there.

"Querida, I didn't say any of that to scare you, but this is the reality of what we're dealing with. In my business, it's always necessary to work with what we know for sure, and hope for the best, instead of putting our head in the sand.

"Someone has been calling and hanging up on your line as a way to cause fear. Now that person has raised the stakes and destroyed your home and personal property. Whoever did this has some sort of vendetta against you. They targeted aspects of your life that obviously mean a lot to you. This is personal for them."

Mercedes leaned back in her chair and looked out into the distance. He knew she was taking a moment to let everything sink in. Inhaling deeply, she closed her eyes for a few moments before opening them and turning her attention back to Raul.

When she looked back at him, the fear that was there before was replaced by anger. The trembling in her hand all but stopped.

"Who the hell is doing this?" she asked pointedly.

The left side of Raul's mouth kicked up into a half smile. *There's my Mercedes.* Her usual confidence and fire were returning.

Raul decided to ignore the fact that he'd just thought of Mercedes as "his." Right now, they had work to do.

"That's what we're going to find out. I've already called my top security guy, and he's working on questioning your neighbors. I'll contact him later to see if he can get the phone records to access a number for the hang up calls.

"We need to compile a list of people you think may have something against you—exes, colleagues, other dancers." He stopped talking when Mercedes turned to him sharply and snatched her hand away.

"You know about my dancing?"

Raul frowned. "You're Devyn's best friend and she is married to my best friend. However, I've never seen you perform."

I'd sure like to see you perform just for me.

He decided it was best to leave that last thought unsaid.

"Was it supposed to be a secret?" He wondered why she seemed upset by the fact he knew she was a burlesque dancer.

"No. No, it's not. I just … didn't know you knew. That's all."

Raul decided to change the subject. "Okay, we also need to plan out your schedule for the next few weeks or months, so you can have someone with you at all times."

She lifted a perfectly arched eyebrow. "Do you think that's necessary?"

Raul nodded. "Yes," he said without hesitation.

"It's just … I mean, you said you're the best and I'm not sure I can afford whatever it is you charge."

Raul squeezed the hand he still held. "Don't worry about that."

"You say that, but this already seems to be a big use of your resources, and I'm sure you have high-end clients who could afford triple what I can pay you."

Raul stared at Mercedes. She was right about being able to afford his usual rates. He meant what he said when he told her that he was the best, and the best did not come cheap, but he had no intention of charging Mercedes for anything.

He'd handled security for pro bono clients before. His company did very well with wealthy clients, and he could afford to take on a lot more pro bono clients if he chose. However, this was different. This was Mercedes, and as sure as he had breath in his body, he knew he would do anything to ensure her safety.

"You're Devyn's best friend and the godmother of my godsons. As far as I'm concerned, you're family. We won't discuss cost. Let me think about that. Right now, we have to worry about keeping you safe," he said, looking her directly in the eyes to let her know he was serious.

After a few heartbeats she nodded.

"Okay. So will this person be at my apartment? It may be a few days or even weeks before I can go back there."

Raul sighed heavily as he stopped listening to what she was saying. He knew she was not going to like what he was about to say. "You're not going back to your apartment."

"What do you mean?" Mercedes asked, her brown eyes leveling a glare at him.

"I mean, your apartment isn't safe, so to ensure your safety, you're going to stay with me, at my home." Raul wanted to grin at the challenge he saw in her expression.

He wouldn't waste his breath informing her that this was a battle she wouldn't win. He quite liked seeing her defiant side.

"Hell no! If you think you can use this as a shot to get me in your damn bed, then you have another thing coming!" she insisted before pushing back in her chair to stand.

Raul reached out, placing a hand on her thigh. Mercedes was wearing a pair of black, high waist shorts, so his hand made contact with her skin. Feeling the supple skin of her thigh beneath his palm, his heart pulsed with an electrified energy.

Now that the fear was mostly gone from Mercedes, it seemed his body's attraction to her returned in full force.

Mercedes sat back in her chair as she looked at his hand on her thigh, and Raul left his hand right where it was.

"Mercedes, it's obvious we both have an attraction for one another. You like me, but you're scared to admit it." He leaned in closer. "We both know I don't have to come up with some elaborate ass excuse to get you into my bed." Letting his words sink in, he squeezed her thigh with the hand that still rested on it.

"With that said, I have four bedrooms, a top rate security system, and I live in a gated community. No one is breaking into my home. You'll be safe there."

From your stalker, that is.

Raul wouldn't question himself as to why he wanted Mercedes to stay in his home. He never let any other client stay in his house. It was evident that his desire to protect Mercedes went well beyond professional courtesy.

Mercedes huffed and crossed her arms over her breasts. "Well damn, aren't you the charmer?" she asked mockingly, unable to deny his claim.

Smiling, Raul squeezed her thigh one final time before letting it go.

"You already know the answer to that, querida." His smile deepened at the sight of Mercedes biting her lower lip. He was having as much of an affect on her as she was on him.

Good.

"There's nowhere else for you to go. Your apartment is a mess and unsafe, Devyn and Nikola are leaving in a week to spend the summer in Brazil, and you'd be here all alone. And I'm not about to allow you to remain here alone."

Mercedes turned her gaze to his eyes. "Did you just say 'allow' me? You're not going to allow me—"

Here we go, Raul thought. He raised his hand to cut off her impending tirade.

"Poor choice of words. Look, it's better for you to stay with me, so we can work together to find whoever is behind this, while keeping you safe. Don't let your stubbornness get in the way of your safety," he said seriously.

She knew as well as he did what he said was the truth. Nikola and Devyn were going to spend most of their summer at their home in Brazil. Though Mercedes was scheduled to travel to different performances throughout the summer, when she was home in Atlanta she would be here alone.

Mercedes let out a breath as she ran a hand through her hair, which she'd styled in a twist out that she had pinned up in a high, curly puff.

"You have four bedrooms?" Mercedes eyed him suspiciously.

Raul could tell she was acquiescing. He nodded. "Yes. Well, three … aside from the master bedroom. You will have complete privacy. If you want it."

He let that final statement hang in the air and watched as Mercedes sighed.

For the next fifteen minutes Raul and Mercedes discussed their living arrangement and her travel schedule over the next few months. Mercedes had big performances in three major cities along with performances at The Black Kitty and smaller cities.

This summer, like most of her others, were busy. Raul decided that he would travel with her to her performances. He'd begin making the travel arrangements in the morning, since her New York performance was the following week. A little while later Devyn and Nikola returned, and they spent another hour catching up and talking, before Raul got a call from one of his employees.

Lorenzo informed Raul of his findings at Mercedes' apartment. Raul wanted to wait until he was alone with Mercedes to update her. He also needed to talk to her to compile a list of names of who could be behind this. He'd have his team start talking to suspects on the list over the next few days.

Raul and Mercedes left later that afternoon. Instead of going directly to Raul's home, they made a stop at a few costume and linen stores. Mercedes wanted to begin replacing some of the costumes she'd lost in the break-in. She told him that she made most of her costumes by hand, and she wanted to spend the next week repairing the damage to her costumes or making new ones to perform in.

They stopped by her apartment, and Mercedes managed to collect a few items that managed to escape total annihilation, including some of the beads and accessories. It was at her apartment Raul had to tell her his team discovered her car tires had been slashed. Raul had already made the arrangements to have her car towed and the tires fixed.

They waited for the tow company to show up and take Mercedes' insurance information.

By the time they got back to Raul's home, it was eight o'clock that evening. With her shoulders slumped, Mercedes appeared as if she felt the weight of the last few days had finally begun to wear on her. Raul took her bags up to one of the guest rooms and told her to settle down in his living room.

After ordering some takeout, he decided to make her a drink while they waited.

Raul went out to his back patio and picked two limes from his potted lime trees and brought them to the kitchen. He quartered the limes and mashed them together with sugar and poured in the cachaca, making his favorite Brazilian drink.

After pouring the drink over ice and adding lime slices to each glass, he walked over to Mercedes who was seated on his L-shaped sectional sofa. Mercedes had the world news channel on, but she wasn't paying attention to the screen.

"Food is on its way," he said to grab her attention. He handed her the glass. "I figured you needed this."

Although he saw her raise a questioning eyebrow, he proceeded with lifting his hand with the other glass in cheers and took a sip of his own drink.

"Mmmmm," Mercedes moaned, as she closed her eyes.

Raul's dick twitched at the sound and the satisfied expression on her face.

"That's delicious. What is it?" Mercedes asked, peeling her eyes open to look at him.

For a second their eyes locked, and Raul felt like he'd been struck by a lightning bolt. He watched as she licked the remnants of the drink from her lips, her tongue flickering at the corner of her mouth.

Biting back a groan, he shook his head to get those thoughts out of his mind. He knew he shouldn't be thinking of Mercedes this way. Not right now. She needed his security expertise first, not his lusty thoughts.

He cleared his throat. "It's called Caipirinha, Brazil's most popular drink." He took another sip, needing the ice-cold liquid to cool his libido down.

"Thank you. This is excellent," she said before taking another sip, and closing her eyes once again. She looked as if the drink was helping her relax.

Raul's phone buzzed. It was the security gate letting him know the takeout had arrived.

Just in time, Raul thought as he went to retrieve the Chinese takeout he'd ordered. They ate mostly in silence.

After finishing her meal, Mercedes turned to Raul. "I, uh … I just wanted to say thank you for all of this."

Raul saw the sincere look of appreciation in her eyes and couldn't help the protective urge that came over him. He stood, moved around the table, and brushed his lips across her forehead.

He stilled at the heat that raced through his body. He forced himself not to take her in his arms, because from the sigh that broke free from Mercedes lips, he knew she would've allowed him to.

"Querida, you don't have to thank me," he said sincerely. "You need help and I'm more than capable of helping. I'll put the rest of the food away."

Raul nudged his head in the direction of the stairs. "You can head up to your room. It's the second door on the right. All your bags are in there, and it has its own fully stocked bathroom. Let me know if you need anything."

She gave him a smile. "Thank you."

He peered at her through half closed eyelids as she ascended the stairs. Watching the sway of her hips and the way the fabric of her shorts gripped her behind, he blew out a breath.

It's gonna be a cold shower for me tonight, he thought.

CHAPTER 8

Mercedes laid in bed, restless. It was just after six in the morning, and even though she had nowhere she needed to be, she couldn't sleep any longer.

It'd been two days since Raul brought her to his home, and so far he was a perfect gentleman. Together they compiled a list of her recent exes, colleagues, and anyone else she could think of who might be behind this. Truthfully, Mercedes didn't think anyone she knew would do something like this. However, Raul strongly believed it was someone she knew or had come in contact with somewhere.

His security team started gathering information on everyone on the list and would soon begin contacting them for questioning. For her part, Mercedes busied herself repairing or re-creating her burlesque costumes. She was bummed that most of her costumes had been destroyed, but she loved doing arts and crafts and the sewing, gluing, and piecing together of her costumes.

Mercedes had developed an enjoyment for arts and crafts as a child when her mother started a children's daycare at her father's church. She would help the children with their creations and designs. She carried this enjoyment with her in both her teaching and in her own apartment.

She often created arts and crafts projects as assignments for her students, and much of her own furniture and decorations around her apartment she either made by hand or had refurbished.

When she discovered burlesque, she found yet another way to indulge in her love for crafts by designing her own costumes.

Sighing, Mercedes sat up in bed and placed her feet on the floor. She thought about Raul. Just the thought of him brought a smile to her face. She was surprised when she entered his home two nights before. She was sure she would find the typical, sparsely decorated bachelor pad.

That was not the case.

Though the home did scream "single male" with its dark-colored furniture and huge, flat screen television, it was still inviting. He had pictures of family members, including his two godsons, throughout the living room.

Mercedes was also pleasantly surprised when she saw the guest room she was staying in was fully equipped with a king size bed, chaise lounge, closet, and dressers. A large bay view window allowed her a complete view of his spacious backyard.

As he told her that first night, she had her own fully stocked bathroom so she didn't have to worry about sharing or running into him while only dressed in a towel.

Not that I'd mind. Mercedes' smile grew larger imagining running into Raul with only a towel wrapped around his waist. She could picture his golden skin as water dripped down what she was sure was a very defined six pack of abs.

Blinking, Mercedes tried to clear her mind. She needed to remind herself she wasn't here for that. She was in his home because someone was stalking her. There was a very real threat against her, and she couldn't afford to get caught up fantasizing about Raul.

She stood and walked to the bathroom to brush her teeth, deciding to do a short workout before heading downstairs. She figured she would have enough time to work out and then make breakfast before Raul came down as a small token of her appreciation for his help.

Mercedes finished brushing her teeth, pulled her hair up in a high bun, and threw on a pair of black workout leggings and a hot pink T-shirt.

After finding one of her favorite kickboxing routines on YouTube, she kicked, punched, and sweated for the next forty-five minutes. Feeling energized by her workout, she showered, put her hair in a goddess braid, and moisturized her skin before putting on a long, sleeveless sundress.

Heading downstairs to the kitchen, Mercedes peeked down the hall at the door to Raul's bedroom and found it was closed. She figured he was still sleeping. He'd told her he didn't need to go into the office until later that day.

Mercedes made her way into his kitchen, and once again, she found herself in love with the large space and Italian marble counter-tops. She loved to cook, and she'd learned in the last few days that Raul knew his way around the kitchen as well. His kitchen appliances could rival those of any top chef.

Mercedes grabbed some eggs, veggies, and fruit to start breakfast. She didn't eat meat except for fish and seafood, and Raul had made sure to stock his refrigerator with plenty of foods she could eat. She made two veggie omelets, cut fruit to make a fruit salad, and placed some whole grain bread in the toaster.

While the bread toasted, she headed upstairs to see if Raul was awake. It was getting close to eight o'clock, so she assumed he was up. She found the door to his bedroom was still closed, and after she rapped on it a few times, she heard nothing.

Right before she turned to leave, movement out of the corner of her eye caught her attention. Farther down the hall, a door was opened, and she heard low music playing. Mercedes had assumed this room was another bedroom, but as she got closer, she realized it had been converted into a gym.

In the middle of the room, Mercedes saw Raul dressed in only a pair of dark gray workout shorts. His back was to her, as he kicked high and swooped down close to the floor. He crouched and spun, twisting and contorting his body.

At first glance, seeing his kicks, Mercedes thought he was doing some sort of kickboxing, but it was nothing she was familiar with.

His moves were as light and graceful as a gazelle, but she could tell his kicks held the power of a sledgehammer. He swept one leg under the other, before leaping on his back and jumping into a crouched position.

She knew it took years to develop that type of skill and dexterity.

The music in the background was a mix of chanting and hand drums. Though she didn't understand the words, she felt the beat vibrate through her body. Raul's movements were in time with the music, making it look like a dance at times instead of kickboxing.

Mercedes was in awe.

She continued to gawk in silence for long minutes, forgetting about the reason she'd come to find Raul in the first place. When he turned around, she could see he was covered in a light sheen of sweat, as if he'd been at this for a long time. Possibly even before she went down to make breakfast.

Mercedes watched a bead of sweat glide down his moist chest, and over the peaks and valleys of his ripped abs.

Just as she'd imagined, not an ounce of fat could be found on his body. She unconsciously licked her lips. She was so mesmerized by that one bead of sweat, she didn't realize he'd stopped moving to watch her as well.

Mercedes was pulled out of her reverie when he cleared his throat. Her eyes flew to his face, and she saw the knowing smile that rested there. Her belly warmed at that mischievous smile. Mercedes decided to forego her embarrassment.

Heck, the man already knew she was attracted to him.

So what if he caught her gawking?

"Good morning. I came up to see if you were awake. I prepared breakfast if you're hungry," she told him, struggling to not let her eyes trail down the rest of his body.

Raul moved to the side of the room, picking up a towel. He wiped his face and chest down before responding.

"Thank you. I'll take a quick shower and be down in a little while."

"Great," was all Mercedes said before she turned and headed back downstairs. She placed the eggs in the oven to keep them warm and grabbed plates and glasses to take out to the back patio. In his backyard, Raul had a massive overhead deck, fully decorated with a large wicker couch and table. The area was surrounded with potted palms and lime and lemon trees.

Mercedes saw it the first morning she'd been at Raul's and fell in love with the area.

Since then, they'd eaten breakfast on the patio—if he was there—or she ate out there alone. She'd asked him how he had citrus trees in Atlanta, and he told her he had a professional gardener teach him to care for them. Once the temperature dipped below fifty degrees, he brought the trees inside in a heated room on the first floor.

There, they kept pretty well until early spring and he could place them back outside. Mercedes loved the ability to have fresh lime and lemons right at her fingertips. She'd already made a couple pitchers of fresh lemonade and asked Raul to teach her to make the drink he made for her on the first night she was there.

She went back to the kitchen to retrieve the fruit and toast, when she heard Raul's footsteps coming down the stairs. He came over to help her carry the rest of their breakfast out, then went back in to grab the orange juice and start the coffeemaker.

Mercedes wasn't much of a coffee drinker, but after one taste of the special Brazilian blend he'd brought from home she'd been converted.

The rich, smooth coffee was unlike any other cup of coffee she had before.

"This looks great. Thanks for cooking," Raul commented as they sat down to eat.

"No problem." Mercedes wanted to ask him about what she saw him doing in the workout room earlier. She hadn't meant to intrude on his workout, but he had looked so fluid and graceful. His body was like poetry in motion. She couldn't help but stare at him as he moved.

They made small talk about the day's plan for a little while, before Mercedes decided to ask him about it.

"What were you doing in the workout room?" she asked, then popped a piece of cantaloupe in her mouth.

He sat back in his seat as a thoughtful expression passed over his face. "It's called capoeira."

She swallowed her fruit. "Capoeira," she repeated. "It's beautiful, but what is it? I mean, it looks like you were doing some type of martial art, but dancing at the same time."

Raul nodded as he chewed and swallowed the bite of eggs he'd just forked into his mouth. He wiped his mouth before speaking. "It is."

Mercedes must have looked confused, because he smiled and explained, "It's both, actually. It's a martial art disguised as a dance."

"Really?" Mercedes asked, intrigued.

"Yup."

"How did you learn it?" She moved to the edge of her seat. He had her interest piqued.

She never knew such a style of fighting existed … not that she was familiar with most martial arts.

Raul seemed just as excited to talk about it as she was in learning. "It's a Brazilian martial art. It was developed by enslaved Africans who were brought over by the Portuguese. Slaves were forbidden to practice their African martial arts, for obvious reasons. The enslavers didn't want the slaves developing a resistance, but they did allow them to get together and practice dancing.

"It was seen as a way to keep their spirits up, which would increase productivity. What they didn't know was that the Africans came up with an ingenious way to disguise their practice of martial arts …"

"They hid it in their dance," Mercedes guessed.

Raul smiled and nodded.

"Wow," she said in awe. "How did you learn it?"

"It was through capoeira that many slaves were able to escape their enslavers and formed groups known as Quilombos. The Quilombos fought against the Portuguese and escaped into the deeper rain forests beyond Portuguese control, creating communities of freed slaves.

"One of the most well-known of these communities is Palmares. My paternal grandmother is a descendant of the people of Palmares.

For years, our family has passed down capoeira from one generation to the next. My grandmother and father taught me when I was really young, and I've been doing it ever since."

Mercedes was amazed as she continued to listen to the story Raul shared with her. She'd known that Brazil had been involved in the slave trade, but she'd never heard of the resistance of the slaves, or of Capoeira. She was enraptured as Raul shared his family history with her and the bond he shared with this grandmother who taught him all about their family's history.

She could see the admiration he held for his grandmother, and the passion he had about the topic of his family history. Mercedes learned that Raul, like many Brazilians, was a mix of Afro-Latino, Indigenous, and Portuguese. She wanted to ask Raul to teach her, but didn't know if it was something that he was willing to share with someone who wasn't family.

They continued to eat and talk for a while longer, before Raul checked the time. It was after nine-thirty. They'd spent an hour and a half talking about his family, dancing, and capoeira. Mercedes had shared with him her love of dancing and how she got started in burlesque.

Though, she'd clammed up when he asked about her family.

Her family didn't know this side of her. Her father would not like that she performed half naked in front of a live audience and would refer to her as some kind of whore. Her grip tightened on her cup as she thought about the ugly words her father would hurl at her if he found out about her burlesque dancing.

"Are you okay?" Raul looked at her with concern in his eyes.

Realizing her emotions were displayed on her face, she pushed the thought of her parents away.

"Yes, I'm fine. Just thinking about the parts of my costume I have to complete before we leave this Thursday."

It was Tuesday, and they were scheduled to leave in two days for New York, where she had performances on Friday, Saturday, and Sunday nights.

Raul's gaze continued to linger on her as if he was trying to figure out if she was telling the truth. Whatever he saw must have convinced him to not push and he dropped the subject.

"It will be fine. I can help you if you need it," he offered.

Mercedes laughed. "Oh yeah, you know how to sew or glue sequins on a corset?"

"Don't underestimate my skills. I'm a man of many talents." He winked at her and gave her his signature smile.

Mercedes felt the butterflies rise in her stomach as she stared into those brown pools he called eyes. Once again, she thought, *This man is beautiful.* She noticed the wrinkling of the outside of his eyes when he smiled. Her gaze moved down to his upturned, full lips. She bit the inside of her cheek to keep from licking her own.

"You're a dangerous man, Raul Santiago," she murmured.

His smile widened while a lascivious glint appeared in his gaze. "In more ways than one, querida."

Mercedes did her best to ignore the way her body warmed at the deep timbre in voice.

"I should get going. Your car is actually scheduled to be done today, so I'll be back early this evening to take you to pick it up," he said as he bent down to pick up the plates.

"I'll get those." Mercedes told him. "And thank you. I'm just going to be working on my costumes for most of the day anyway."

"Oh, Nikola and Devyn invited us to dinner at their place before we leave for New York. I know you're probably getting a little claustrophobic being stuck in here most of the day. We can go over there tonight."

She smiled. "I'd like that."

Truth was, under ordinary circumstances being inside for nearly three days straight would make her want to climb the walls, but she felt comfortable in Raul's home and he'd been good company. But she did want to say good-bye to Devyn before she and Nikola took off for the summer.

Mercedes gathered their breakfast dishes, put them in the kitchen sink, and then walked Raul to the door. He'd taught her how to set the alarm, and once he left, she would put in the security code. As she stood on the front stone steps of his house and watched him fold himself into the driver's seat of his car, she felt something strange course through her.

This felt … natural.

Almost like a wife waving to her husband as he went off to work and she stayed home and tended to the kids.

Mercedes knew that thought was ridiculous.

They weren't married or anywhere close to it. They certainly didn't have any kids. So why was she feeling so comfortable in his space? Why did her heart whisper that this felt right?

Mercedes looked up when she heard Raul's horn blow and he waved as he exited the driveway. She smiled and waved back, then reentered the house, pushing those unexpected notions aside.

Mercedes had no intention of being anyone's wife, or even girlfriend, in the near future.

CHAPTER 9

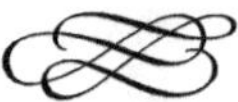

Raul watched as Mercedes moved from the bed, to the chair, back to the bed, and now stood looking out the window. He felt a little guilty for scolding her about not checking the peephole before opening the door for him.

He'd gone down to the front desk soon after they checked in, but he left his key in the room as a test. When he came back up and knocked, he was more than a little angry to find that she opened the door without so much as asking, "Who is it?" Her excuse that she thought it was a hotel employee didn't sit well with him.

Raul had thoroughly reminded her that she was to check *every single time* before opening the door for anyone.

Now that he had a little time to cool off, he recognized how nervous his chastisement must've made her. He wanted to do something to calm her down.

"Do you think this person followed me up here?" she asked, still staring out the window.

Without thinking too much about it, he reached for her, pulling her into his body. He stroked her back, needing to touch her, to both reassure her and himself.

"We don't know," he replied to her question honestly. "It's possible, but nothing is going to happen to you. You're not in this alone."

She pulled back to give him a half smile. "I know. I trust you. It's just that knowing this person could be in the audience, or hell, even one of the dancers, is scary. I love dancing and performing. Usually, I can't wait to hit the stage, but today I feel like I want to do anything but get up there and perform." She stepped out of his hold and moved to sit on the side of the bed.

Raul's heart constricted at seeing the anguish on her face. Knowing this was exactly what her stalker wanted, his core temperature rose. Whoever was behind this wanted Mercedes to feel intimidated and stop doing the things she enjoyed. This was part of stalking. It wasn't just about the physical danger, but the mental and emotional toll it took on the victim.

This was how stalkers got and maintained control of their victims.

Raul took a seat in a chair at the side of the bed and clasped Mercedes' hands in his. "Hey, it's going to be okay. I know you're scared, but you can't give into fear. This is what they want. They want you to become a shell of yourself. You can't give them that control."

He lifted her hands to his lips and kissed each one. Her skin felt so right against his lips. He saw her eyes widen slightly, but she didn't pull away.

"What's something you do to calm yourself before a performance?" he asked.

Mercedes thought for a moment and shrugged. "Truth is, I don't really get nervous anymore. I haven't done anything to prepare me for the stage in a while. But when I first started there was this one thing I did …" She trailed off.

Raul lifted his eyebrow. "What was it?"

"All right, I'll tell you, but if you laugh or try to mock me, I'll kick your ass," she said sternly.

He smiled. "I have no doubt you would try. I promise, querida, I won't laugh. What was it?"

Thirty minutes later, the pair sat on Mercedes' hotel bed eating and watching *The Josephine Baker Story.* Mercedes was enraptured with the film.

Raul preferred to watch Mercedes rather than the movie. He saw every emotion play out on her face. One scene in particular seemed to touch her. It was the scene in which Baker, as played by Lynn Whitfield, completed her first nude photo shoot, and after sleeping with the photographer, she stared at her body in the mirror.

Baker played with her hair, pushing it back out of her face, and turned left and right, examining herself.

Baker's voiceover stated, "There she was." This was when Baker first came to terms with her exhibitionism on stage. This was the turning point in Josephine's career. Raul looked on as Mercedes' eyes lit up like Christmas trees as if she identified with Josephine's story.

He wondered if that was what dancing did for her. Did it give her the opportunity to express her true self?

Never one to let his curiosity go unsatisfied, Raul decided to ask Mercedes about it after the movie ended.

"That scene seemed to really touch you," he stated as the film credits rolled.

"Which scene?"

"The one with her looking in the mirror. Can you relate? Is that how you felt when you started dancing?"

Mercedes lifted an eyebrow as if she was deciding on how much she wanted to tell him. Raul longed to push her, to probe her for more information. He found himself wanting to know more and more about the woman sitting before him. She was a mixture of spitfire, mystery, and recluse. He was good at reading people, and he realized that while she could be very forthcoming, and even blunt, she held something back. He wanted to know how she came to be that way.

Raul needed to break through whatever wall she had up that she used to keep most people at arm's length.

Finally, Mercedes tipped her head. "Yeah, I can relate. When I discovered burlesque, it just felt natural." She shrugged.

Raul lifted an eyebrow when she didn't say anything more. After a minute of silence, he decided to let the topic drop. He knew she wouldn't give up more information, but he was sure there was more to the story.

Raul convinced Mercedes to take a walk around Central Park where they made small talk and enjoyed the scenery. Mercedes' mood lightened up, which was what Raul wanted. He saw the tension release from her shoulders during the movie, and she was able to focus on the reason they were in New York.

He didn't lie when he said he was looking forward to her performance. For the past week, he'd watched her sew and redesign her costumes, and he wanted to see her in the outfits. By the consideration she took in designing he knew she cared deeply about performing and being her best.

He wouldn't let her stalker get in the way of that.

Unbeknownst to Mercedes, he had two of his employees come up to New York and check out the club, and sleep in the same hotel. They would be his backup in the audience tonight in case he needed them.

He wouldn't let anything happen to her.

* * *

MERCEDES FOLLOWED behind Raul as they entered the club. A few patrons mingled about, while most had their full attention on the performer on the stage.

"I'm sorry, sir, but only performers are allowed in this area," the beefy security guard who stood in front of the entryway to the backstage area said.

Mercedes watched as Raul looked the guy up and down, sizing him up. "We're allowed." Raul's tone was clipped.

The guard shook his head and gave a half smirk as if something was funny. "All these fuckers wanna sneak backstage to do their girl in a burlesque club. You got a fetish or something, buddy?"

The mockery in this guy's tone obviously didn't sit well with Raul because he stepped closer, getting in the dude's face.

"I'll let that shit slide only because I don't want to ruin the first opportunity I have to watch Mercedes on stage. But if you don't get your steroid taking ass the hell out of my way, I will put you face-first into the fucking ground."

Mercedes' eyes widened at the growl in Raul's voice.

"Who the—"

"James, he's okay."

Raul and Mercedes turned to see the owner of the club moving in between Raul and the security guard.

"He's fine." The owner patted the guard on the shoulder. "My apologies, Mr. Santiago. I forgot to tell my security that you'd be here this evening."

Raul glared at the security guard and then at the owner. "Just don't let it happen again." He turned to Mercedes and took her hand in his, allowing her to follow him to the private dressing room that he'd requested for her.

"That was intense," Mercedes said when they paused in front of the dressing room door.

Raul didn't say anything as his gaze scoured the rest of the hallway. His shoulders sat a little higher than normal and the tension emanated from his body. She could tell he was in protective mode.

Mercedes did her best to ignore the buzzing in her head and the way her nipples pressed against the pasties she wore, a result of seeing Raul's intensity.

"The room's clear," Raul told her after he quickly checked it over. "You can finish getting dressed."

She nodded and entered the dressing room, glad for a minute of privacy. The closeness between her and Raul was starting to get to her. She could feel herself wanting to open up more and more to him. And she knew with that openness, her heart would follow.

That wasn't something she could allow.

* * *

Twenty minutes after entering the dressing room, Mercedes was ready to take her place onstage.

"This next performer is something of a treat …"

Mercedes stood at the edge of the stage, listening to the emcee make her introduction. She wore a navy blue and purple peacock tutu skirt, thigh-high black leather boots with four-inch heels, a purple corset with peacock feathers on it, a navy blue choker, and her hair pinned up high with a few curls falling around her face.

She opted to go with light makeup; a purple lip, light concealer, and golden eyeshadow completed the costume with black satin gloves. She looked across the stage and saw Raul dressed in dark pants and a short sleeve, button-up, light-colored shirt, with a suit jacket over the top.

At that moment, Raul turned and looked Mercedes directly in the eye and winked. Feeling a quiver in her belly, she dipped her head. Mercedes wasn't typically shy when it came to flirtation of showing her physical attraction, but Raul was different. Because she knew if she weren't careful, Raul could easily become more than just a physical attraction.

She could get lost in those big, brown eyes of his and never want to be found. Mercedes sighed.

Before she could get too lost in thought about her warring emotions about Raul, the emcee, Miss Celia, completed her announcement.

"Welcome to the stage, Black Daaahhhliaaaa!"

The audience clapped and whistled.

The opening notes of Eartha Kitt's "Careless Love" began playing as Mercedes strutted on stage. The live band in the club helped add energy to Mercedes' performance.

She shimmied from left to right, stopping to bite the end of her left glove, and slowly removed her hand before tossing the glove to the side. She repeated the move with the other hand, then turned and presented the audience with her backside, where she lifted the end of her peacock skirt, giving them a view of her round behind.

Mercedes spun and swiveled her hips while tapping her foot to the beat and reaching around to loosen the strings of her corset.

Her body tingled with that familiar rush that came with performing. She gleaned energy from the audience. Her worries about her stalker and her mounting feelings for Raul evaporated. All that mattered was the reaction she drew from the crowd.

Her lips parted in a mischievous smile, and she ran her tongue across her bottom lip while swiveling her hips seductively.

What few people knew was that this song held special meaning for Mercedes. When she first heard it a few years ago, it spoke to her reluctance to fall in love or desire to marry. She'd seen the pain her mother endured because of love. She watched for years as her father repeatedly cheated. She'd even seen other women and friends in her life cry over no good men.

Her own best friend had fallen in love with a man who emotionally abused and cheated on her in the bed they shared. She'd held Devyn as she cried over her ex-boyfriend, and while Devyn was happy now, that situation was another reminder for Mercedes that love was often painful.

Mercedes vowed that would never be her. She never wanted to get that deep with anyone. Not at the expense of her own sanity.

By the time Eartha Kitt ended her lamentations on the sins of loving the wrong man, Mercedes was left in her thong, boots, and navy blue pasties with tassels. She shimmied her shoulders, making the tassels swing, and blew a kiss to the audience.

Before exiting the stage, she glanced over and found Raul's gaze transfixed on her. He was clapping proudly as he let his eyes roam her body. Mercedes felt the heat rise in her body at his perusal. She'd been doing burlesque for years and was no stranger to men openly ogling her body.

She usually enjoyed it, as long as they kept their hands to themselves. However, Raul's look had the ability to make her feel like a schoolgirl having her first crush. Exiting the stage on the same side as Raul, she felt his heated gaze on her as she walked past.

"That was wonderful, querida," he whispered in her ear, before they turned and made their way down the hallway.

"Thank you," was all she said, as she followed him down the hall.

Mercedes didn't want to examine the pride she felt at his compliment. This was only her first performance of two for the night.

She didn't have time to wonder about how Raul made her feel. She needed to get backstage, change into her second costume of the night, and prepare for her final performance.

She entered the changing room, and found her discarded costume already waiting for her.

After packing the costume into her bag, she began removing her second costume from the locker. She had another half an hour before her next performance, so she was in no rush to change. She sat taking off the thigh-high boots, and slid on a pair of fishnet stockings, followed by her long, red skirt. She changed her pasties to a pair of heart-shaped red ones with tassels, and put on a long sleeve, red halter top that buttoned up in the back.

Ordinarily, Mercedes had one of the other girls help her button it, but she was alone. Just as she was wondering how to secure the top, there was a knock on the door.

"Mercedes, it's me," Raul announced through the door.

Mercedes felt her nipples harden at the sound of his voice. She shook her head at her body's response to his voice.

"Just a second!" she yelled through the door.

After quickly slipping her feet into her second pair of four-inch heels for the evening, she walked to the door, opening it slightly to make sure it was Raul. He'd already scolded her once about not being safe enough opening doors, she did not want a repeat of that.

She was in too good a mood.

Performing always gave her the release she needed, and she was still on a high from her earlier performance and couldn't wait to hit the stage for her next one.

Her second performance was to the version of "Candyman" by the Mambo Kings. This was a more upbeat performance than the first and she intended to let her fun, sexy side show.

"Um, I need your help with something," she told him.

"What's that?"

"Could you, uh, help me button this up?" She turned a little so that he could see the buttons that she referred to.

When Mercedes turned back to face him, she spotted the heated look in his eyes. Her nipples grew impossibly harder, and her pussy muscles clenched.

Breathe, girl. Breathe, she reminded herself.

"Turn around." His voice came out huskier than it had been a minute ago. Raul lifted his hand to the buttons of her top and let one of his knuckles lightly trail down the skin of her back.

Mercedes' breathing hitched and she bit her bottom lip.

"You were wonderful out there," he said in her ear, crowding her from behind.

"Thank you," she whispered.

Her skin tingled at the feel of his hands on her body. She bit down on her lip even harder to keep from moaning. A beat later, Mercedes looked up and saw they were facing the full-length mirror and Raul's eyes were on her mouth.

He dragged his eyes up to meet hers, and gave her a smirk, as if he knew what his closeness was doing to her. Mercedes cleared her throat.

"You're all set," he stated as he ran his hands across her shoulders.

Mercedes took a step forward and turned to face him.

"Are you enjoying the show so far?" she asked, moving to put on the rest of her costume accessories. "Aside from the fact you're kind of working?"

"I'm enjoying myself immensely. Never had so much fun on a job before," he said, giving her another sexy smile.

A job? She wondered if that was how he thought of her, all the while avoiding eye contact with him. She shook her head to rid herself of that thought, then continued putting in her gold earrings.

"Good. I'm glad. Is this your first burlesque show ever?"

"No, I've been to a couple before in Brazil and Vegas, but this one is special," he said, giving her a heated look.

Mercedes smiled. "'Cause you're working?"

"No," he replied honestly.

Their eyes locked for a few moments. Mercedes was shocked at the desire Raul openly displayed. She knew his eyes were a mirror of her own, and she quickly turned her head.

"I'll let you finish getting dressed. I just wanted to check on you," he told her before turning and walking to the door. "I'll be right outside of the door if you need anything."

Mercedes took a deep breath when the door closed with Raul on the opposite side. Checking the time, she realized she now only had ten minutes before her next performance. In a rush, she changed her lipstick color to a shiny red lip with a cat-eye in black eyeliner before giving herself one last look in the mirror.

She grabbed the black cane she planned to use for her performance and headed out the door.

Raul greeted her with a smile.

"Ready?" he asked, looking her up and down.

"It's showtime!" she said excitedly, and Raul walked ahead of her, for safety purposes.

Once they arrived at the side of the stage, they both watched as another performer completed her performance. The emcee came up to tell the audience they were taking a five-minute break, and they would return with a very special performance.

That was Mercedes' cue to get in position.

"Good luck, Dahlia!" came a voice from behind.

Mercedes and Raul turned to see a performer from earlier. Essence Almighty was her stage name. She and Mercedes had met numerous times throughout the years, often performing in the same clubs.

"Thank you. You were great, Essence," Mercedes returned.

"Thanks, babe." Essence turned her gaze to Raul, eyeing him up and down lustily. "I don't think we've met. They call me Essence, but you can call me whatever you want," she purred.

Mercedes found herself annoyed at Essence's open flirtation, which she knew was silly. Raul wasn't hers. He was there helping her. Doing a job. Isn't that what he'd called it … a job?

Raul smiled, but Mercedes found herself relieved when she noticed it didn't reach his eyes. "Pleasure. I'm Raul." His tone was more clipped also.

Mercedes let out the breath she unconsciously held.

"Dahlia, where'd you meet this charmer?" Essence asked Mercedes, but kept her eyes on Raul.

"Wouldn't you like to know," Mercedes mumbled.

"I'm sorry?" Essence asked.

"Oh, you know, just on the corner somewhere," Mercedes retorted.

She didn't want to tell Essence that he was actually there for safety reasons. She hadn't told anyone outside of management and the owner of her troubles and wanted to keep it that way. Besides, Raul advised her not to. He believed whoever her stalker was could be someone she met or knew through performing.

The trio heard the emcee return to the stage to begin her introduction.

"It was good seeing you, Dahlia. Good luck. Nice meeting you, Raul," Essence said, winking at him before heading towards the changing room.

"Ladies and gentlemen, put your hands together one more time for the incredible, the illustrious, the unbelievably sexy, Black Dahliaaaaa."

Forgetting all about Essence, Mercedes strutted on stage, clapping her hands to the electric beat of the music. This was her upbeat performance of the night. The rhythm electrified her, and she circled her hips as she spun her back to the audience and shook her ass to the beat. She spun back around and kicked high, allowing the crowd to see her fishnet covered legs.

The claps and shouts increased, further igniting Mercedes' playful side. She raised one side of her skirt and then dropped it, teasing the audience over and over again, before she reached around, unbuttoned the skirt, and let it slide down her firm legs. Kicking the skirt to the side, she dropped down to the stage, spread eagle, and lifted and ground her hips to the beat, earning more applause from the audience.

She stood and swiveled her hips, then reached around to undo the buttons at the back of her crop top. Slowly, she unbuttoned them one by one, and teased the audience some more as she stepped across the stage, ripping off the shirt, and tossing it to the side.

Mercedes bent at the waist, rotating her backside, before whipping her head back and coming up slowly, revealing her pasty-clad breasts and shaking them for the crowd to end the routine.

She blew a kiss to the crowd and took a final bow.

Mercedes exited the opposite side of the stage as Raul. She felt light as the adrenaline rush from her performance continued. Mercedes floated down the hallway. Out of the corner of her eye, she noticed Raul walking behind her.

She smiled when she entered her private changing room, humming to herself, and closed the door.

After removing her boots and fishnet stockings, she put on a long, flowy, gray skirt, removed her pasties, and donned a black, gray, and white V-neck T-shirt. Just as she was finishing changing a knock on her door alerted her.

"It's your costume," Raul yelled through the door.

"Thank you," Mercedes said. She pulled the door open and retrieved her garments from him.

After quickly packing, she was ready to head out in a matter of minutes.

She had another performance the following night, and it was after eleven. She was ready to get back to the hotel, bathe, and get into bed.

"Ready to head out or did you want to watch the rest of the show?" Raul asked as she opened the door.

"I'm ready to go, unless you want to stay?"

"I'm good. Let's go," he said, putting his hand on the small of her back.

They had taken a car to the club, and were taking one back to the hotel, which was only about a fifteen-minute drive. Once they got to the hotel, Raul escorted Mercedes to her room and took her keycard to open the door.

Sliding the key into the door, he told Mercedes to wait, while he checked the room as a precaution. Mercedes peeked in the room as he turned the lights on and carefully checked all the corners and even under the bed.

She admired how his muscles bunched and tightened under his

clothing. With the adrenaline from performing still coursing through her, she could feel herself growing hot with arousal as she licked her lips.

At that precise moment, Raul turned to see her eyeing him. He waved her in the room, letting her know it was safe, then moved to stand in front of her.

"You were really great tonight," he said in a low voice.

"Did I live up to my reputation?" she asked playfully.

"You exceeded it."

He lifted his hand to sweep a curl behind her ear.

His light touch sent chills through Mercedes' body.

Tonight, Raul had fought with everything inside of him not to grab Mercedes off of that stage. Ordinarily, he didn't consider himself a jealous man, but damn it if he didn't want to bash in the skull of every man who was in the audience at that club.

He'd fought like hell to maintain some sort of professional distance, but now that he had her alone, the need to have her writhing body beneath him took over his common sense.

He yanked her body into his, causing Mercedes to gasp. "Do you know how fucking sexy you are?" His voice came out as a growl.

Mercedes shook her head. "Tell me."

Raul chose not to use his words. Instead, he palmed the back of her head, bringing her lips to his.

The kiss took Mercedes back to the first time they'd done this, in a different hotel.

She felt his tongue on her lips, nudging her lips open. When she parted her lips on a sigh, Raul's tongue explored her mouth. Mercedes' eyes drifted closed as she allowed him to plunder her mouth. His hold tightened in her hair.

Mercedes' hands slid around his waist as he pressed himself even closer into her body.

She felt his hands move down her back to cup her ass, pulling her closer to his growing arousal. Mercedes moved her hands up to Raul's head, pulling him tighter against her lips and pressing her breasts against his chest. Raul began walking her backwards toward the bed. Before she knew it, the back of Mercedes' knees hit the bed.

Raul continued to kiss a path down the column of Mercedes' neck. She grabbed the front of his button-down shirt and pulled him down on top of her as she collapsed to the bed. His weight on top of her felt right. Raul placed kisses on the sides of Mercedes' mouth, before moving down to her neck and the tops of her breasts.

His progress was impeded by her thin T-shirt. Moving lower, he pushed the shirt up, exposing soft, dark brown skin. He placed kisses down her stomach, stopping to dip his tongue in her belly button. Mercedes moaned and arched into his kiss.

Apparently, Raul needed more. He slid down her body, pulling her long skirt as he went, exposing the black, lacy thong she wore underneath.

"Fuck," he swore under his breath.

Seeing her on stage nearly nude was one thing, but having her this close, feeling her supple skin, and hearing the hitch of her breath as he placed his hand on the top of her panty-clad mound, drove his desire higher than ever.

"Raul," she groaned as if he was the only thing in the world that mattered.

Fuck, Raul thought as he tore away the fabric of her panties.

He spread her legs, opening her up for his perusal. His mouth watered at the pink and swollen lips before him. Never one to turn down a meal, Raul leaned in and licked her pussy lips.

At the first swipe of his tongue, Mercedes instinctively raised her hips, urging him on.

The taste of her juices on his tongue had Raul moaning. She tasted like honey and everything that was right with the world. He wanted more. Raul lost all patience, and began swirling his tongue around her lips, moving up to her clit.

When he wrapped his lips around her clit, Mercedes moaned loudly, moving her hips and pushing her pussy into his face.

Raul obliged by wrapping his arms underneath her thighs and pulling her farther into his face.

Raul began sucking in earnest. Mercedes hands moved up to cup her breasts. Pushing her bra and T-shirt out of the way, she pinched and plucked at her nipples. Her hips had a mind of their own as they jerked, trying to get as close to Raul's mouth as possible. When she felt Raul slide a finger into her wet core, she cried out in sweet agony.

"Ahhh, that feels so fucking good," she panted, just as Raul inserted a second finger. She felt him curl his fingers inside of her as his mouth sucked even harder on her clit. The contact with her G-spot and the pressure on her clit had her orgasm sending waves of pleasure through her body. Her hips moved on their own accord, and Raul continued to suck her through it all.

Mercedes released her breasts, dropping her arms by her sides as she let her breath return to normal. Raul crawled back up her body and rested his weight on his elbows, staring down at Mercedes.

"You taste delectable," he said, his voice thick with arousal.

He pressed a kiss to her parted lips. Mercedes immediately opened her mouth wider, tasting herself on his tongue. Licking his bottom lip, she sucked it into her mouth, nibbling at it before letting go. Raul pulled back, staring into her eyes. She saw a range of emotions behind those beautiful brown eyes of his.

Lust, desire, hesitance.

It was all there before he blinked and they were all gone.

"I want you to come somewhere with me tomorrow," he said.

"Where?"

He shook his head. "You'll find out once we get there."

She eyed him cautiously, wondering where he wanted to take her. And more importantly, why he had stopped. She could feel his thick erection against her thigh. She knew he was turned on. She also knew by the gleam in his eyes that he really wanted her to say yes to his request.

At that moment, Mercedes wanted nothing more than to make Raul happy.

She nodded. "Sure, why not?"

Raul's eyes lit up, as if wherever he was taking her had special meaning to him.

He pressed another kiss to her lips. "Be ready by nine thirty tomorrow morning."

His eagerness pleased Mercedes.

"Okay."

Slowly, Raul raised himself up off the bed. He turned to take one last look at Mercedes, naked on the bed. Never shy about her nudity, she reveled in the desire she saw burning in his eyes. Allowing her gaze to sweep down his body to the bulge in his pants, she smiled.

"I'll let you turn in. Just knock on the door if you need anything," he said, gesturing to the door that separated their two rooms.

"Don't forget to put the chain on," he reminded her as he pulled the door closed.

After a few minutes, Mercedes got up, put the chain on, and locked the door. Caught somewhere between wishing Raul hadn't stopped them from fucking and being grateful he had, she sighed.

She now knew that Raul's mouth wasn't only useful for charming the pants off a woman, but just as efficient in making sure a woman was happy she took her pants off to begin with.

She didn't know where this was going with Raul, but she knew if she wasn't careful she would end up in over her head.

Raul awakened the next morning with a smile on his face. He'd had a hell of a time getting to sleep last night. After leaving Mercedes' room, he took a long, cold shower, rubbing one out while he was in there. When he came, the image of Mercedes—with her head thrown back and lips slightly parted as she silently screamed when her orgasm washed over her—appeared in his mind.

It was a memory he would never forget as long as he lived. He hadn't had any intention of going that far with her last night, but watching her be so uninhibited on stage made his dick rock hard. He'd wanted to rip her off that stage and hide her away from any other man, but the sheer look of joy on her face while she danced was enough to keep his jealousy in check.

But after the show, he wanted to make her entirely his. He wanted to feel and share something with her that no one in that audience would be able to. However, he stopped before fully possessing her. He wanted to make sure the first time they had sex it wasn't because she was hopped up on adrenaline from performing.

He would take her for the first time when she had a clear head.

The audience may have the ability to see her beautiful body on stage, but he wanted her more than the Black Dahlia. He wanted to get to know Mercedes, beyond the stage presence. Today he was taking her to a place he went to whenever he had time while visiting the City. After getting up, showering, and dressing in a pair of loose-fitting jeans and a dark, short-sleeve Polo shirt, he ordered breakfast for him and Mercedes.

Next, he knocked on the door that separated their room, checking to see if she was awake.

"Good morning." Mercedes smiled as she opened the door. She was dressed in a pair of jean shorts and a white V-neck. Raul openly allowed his eyes to trail down her smooth as silk skin and gawk at her cleavage.

"Morning," he greeted.

"I wasn't sure what to wear. This okay?" she asked.

"It's perfect. I ordered breakfast. It should be here in another fifteen minutes. Then we can eat and head out."

"Breakfast? We can't eat on the way to wherever we're going? Which, you still haven't told me exactly where that is, by the way." Mercedes eyed him suspiciously, with her hand on her hip.

Raul found himself amused at the intimidating posture she tried to take, but didn't let it show.

"It's a surprise," he said, placing a quick kiss on her cheek, unable to resist touching her any longer. "Don't worry, I'll have you back long before your performance tonight," he promised.

A knock at the door halted Mercedes' response.

"That's probably breakfast. They're early today. We'll eat, then go."

After Raul checked the room service attendant's credentials and the food, he allowed him in the room to set up the table. The pair ate breakfast in Raul's room, making small talk. Thirty minutes later the two were heading out of the door. Raul steered Mercedes to the subway.

"Where we're going is only a few stops away."

Mercedes shrugged and didn't move away when he circled her waist with his arm and guided her down the subway steps.

"So you're still not telling me where we're going, huh?" she questioned again.

Raul smiled. "That would spoil the surprise, querida. How did you sleep?"

Mercedes' lips spread into a dreamy smile, remembering her blissful sleep and what transpired right before she fell asleep.

"I slept like a baby," she purred, opting to leave out the part where she dreamt about the feel of his lips on her, hard muscles covered in golden skin, and the sexiest smile she'd ever seen on a man.

"Good." He smiled down at her, placing a kiss just beneath her ear. "This is us." Raul grabbed Mercedes hand, doing his best to ignore the small jolt of electricity that shot through him at the contact.

He pulled her off the subway and up the subway stairs to keep her close to him in the crowd of exiting passengers. Though they were making a social visit, he never forgot for one second that he was with her because someone was stalking her.

Mercedes' safety was always in the forefront of his mind.

"It's just a block up ahead," he said as they emerged from the subway underground.

Mercedes strained to look ahead, trying to gain some sort of insight into where they were going. When they finally arrived, Raul saw the left side of Mercedes' luscious lips kick up into a half smile.

"Seriously?" she asked excitedly. They stood under a large sign that read "Arte Capoeira" in bold, black letters with images of the Brazilian flag around it.

"My cousin, Francisco, grew up here, and opened this studio about five years ago. I come whenever I'm in the City and have time," he told her.

Usually, the studio was closed on Sundays to most students. But Raul knew Francisco routinely invited a few of his students and friends to the studio on Sunday mornings just to enjoy a light practice.

Raul had been to more than a few of these sessions and wanted to bring Mercedes with him. Just as Raul went to press the buzzer to be let in, the door flew open.

"Primo! I thought that was you." Francisco's voice held a note of laughter and surprise as he pulled Raul into a bear hug. "I didn't know you were in the City," Francisco said as he let Raul go.

Raul stepped back. "It's only for a short trip." He pulled Mercedes to his side. "Primo, this is a friend of mine. She's interested in capoeira, and I thought she could sit in on today's session."

Francisco's hazel eyes widened when he noticed Mercedes standing at Raul's side. "A friend, huh?" he asked, taking Mercedes' hand and pressing his lips to it for a kiss. "Any friend of Raul's is a friend of mine." He winked at Mercedes as she smiled brightly.

"I see flirting runs in the family," she said.

Raul grunted as he took Mercedes' hand, removing it from his cousin's hold. "That's enough."

Francisco raised an eyebrow, a slow, knowing grin spreading across his lips.

"It's a pleasure to meet you, Francisco," Mercedes said, breaking up the tension between the cousins, her hand still firmly in Raul's.

Francisco gave Mercedes another seductive grin. "Oh, the pleasure's all mine, minha linda."

Raul glared at his cousin. "Are you going to let us in?" he asked, more forceful than his normal tone.

"Come. Come in. The others will be here shortly." Francisco waved them in and up the stairs to the large room where they would practice.

While the trio talked, Raul explained to Mercedes there were only five to ten people who showed up on Sundays to practice and hang out. Usually, they all would go to lunch at a nearby Brazilian restaurant afterwards.

They often practiced for a minimum of two hours or so, working up a good sweat and appetite. Raul told her they didn't have to stay the whole time if she didn't want to, or go for lunch, but she didn't mind. Raul could see the intrigue on her face, as she looked at the pictures on the wall and the hand drums that lay in the far corner of the room.

About five minutes later more people began to stroll in, and Francisco handed Raul a pair of pants and a T-shirt to practice in. He had to ask Francisco to lock up the gun he carried with him in the back safe while they practiced. When Francisco eyed him questioningly, Raul told him he was on a job and his cousin dropped it. Francisco knew what Raul did for a living, and that sometimes it required the use of firearms.

Raul took the pair of pants and T-shirt Francisco offered him for Mercedes and turned to take the clothing to her. He found her staring at one of his favorite pictures in the studio. "That's a picture of Mestre Araujo."

In the photo, a brown-skinned woman who appeared to be in her mid-to-late forties looked as if she was standing on one hand as her other hand protected her face, and her legs were in a split position above her head. It was a common capoeira stance.

Mestre Araujo was one of the great female capoeira instructors to rise out of the Brazilian favelas. She was also Raul and Francisco's great-grandmother. The picture had been taken in the 1940s and preserved overtime.

Francisco had hung it up in his studio as a way to pay tribute to his ancestors that passed down the art of capoeira through the family lineage.

Mercedes jumped. "You scared me," she scolded him before taking the clothing Raul offered her.

"She's beautiful. She looks so strong. Did you know her?" she asked.

Raul nodded. "She's our great-grandmother. She passed when I was ten, but she's the one who began teaching me Capoeira," he said proudly.

"That's amazing. I bet she's proud of you and your cousin for continuing on with her teachings."

Raul's chest warmed in satisfaction at Mercedes' words.

"There's a changing room in the back. We're starting in another five minutes or so. You don't have to participate, but Francisco grabbed these just in case you wanted to try your hand at it later on."

Mercedes nodded and told him she'd change into the clothing in case she decided to participate.

Forty minutes later, Raul found himself fully immersed in a capoeira class. He felt exhilarated as the rhythm of the hand drums played out, and he and Francisco were surrounded by the other students, who clapped in time with the drums.

Raul's heartbeat sped up as he spun, kicked, and jumped to avoid Francisco's precise kicks. He ducked and pivoted to counter Francisco's moves.

His cousin loved to show off in front of an audience. However, Raul was no slouch and he kept up with everything Francisco threw at him, countering with a few moves of his own.

No harsh contact was made in their show-off, as this was only a practice.

Whenever Raul or Francisco left themselves exposed to an assault, the other let them know with a light kick or touch, as if to say, *I could have gotten you there, if I wanted.*

In turn, the students surrounding them would clap or utter "ohs" and "ahs" to let the two know they saw the opening as well. Out of the corner of his eye, Raul saw Mercedes dressed in the traditional white pants and T-shirt with the school's logo on it. She clapped in time with the music like the others. On occasion, he saw a worried expression pass over her face when it looked like Francisco would make contact. He sent her a wink to let her know it was okay.

He secretly enjoyed the fact she seemed worried about him. He wanted to tell her he'd been practicing capoeira almost as long as he'd been walking. Even Francisco couldn't knock Raul off his game.

After that set ended, Raul and Francisco stepped out of the circle and let two other students take over where they left off.

"What do you think?" he asked Mercedes as he worked to catch his breath.

"I think that was fabulous," she said close to his ear, so he could hear her over the crowd. "You two look like you've been doing this since birth.".

"We have, pretty much. You want to give it a try?" he asked. When Mercedes looked like she wanted to say no, he grabbed her hand. "It's okay, querida. No one expects you to do any flips or spin on your head. We'll start out with the basics."

For the next hour, the class broke out into partners, where each member was able to practice their skills. Raul taught Mercedes the basic move known as the *ginga*. From the outside it appeared to be simple, when one arm was brought up to protect the face, while the opposite leg steps back.

"It's just like dancing," Raul assured Mercedes when she hesitated. "Let me show you." He held out his hand for her.

When she took it, he pulled her over to one of the far corners of the room. Placing a quick kiss to her knuckles before releasing her, he positioned his body in a crouching position.

"Stand like this."

Mercedes observed and then complied, crouching next to him. Raul then swept his left foot back and around before repositioning into the crouched position. Without his needing to say it, Mercedes followed suit, repeating the movement. Raul then did the same with his right leg, and Mercedes copied his body's flow with her own.

"That's it," Raul crooned as he stood straight, looking down on her. He moved behind her. "Keep it going." He clasped either side of her waist with his hands, helping to steady her.

In all honesty, there was no need for him to touch her. Mercedes' movements were fluid and graceful. But he'd be damned if he could pass up this opportunity to put his hands on her.

"Let's try some kicks," he said after a few rounds of practicing the *ginga*.

Her kicks were high and quick, causing Raul to laugh at how easily she picked up his cultural dance and self-defense moves.

"This is fun. Feels like a night at kickboxing class," Mercedes declared with a huge smile on her face. She came to a stop directly in front of Raul when he spun her around by the waist to face him.

He let his hand hold her in place. Her breathing was slightly erratic, and he briefly let his eyes drop to watch the rise and fall of her breasts. He bit back a groan.

"We should take it easy. You have a performance tonight," he said, not wanting to tire her out too much before her show that evening.

"You're right." Mercedes dipped her head.

Raul regretfully pulled back, letting his hands drop to his sides. The things he wanted to do to this woman he didn't want an audience for. He had to force himself to take a step back.

At the end of class, he and Mercedes accompanied Francisco and the group to a local Brazilian eatery. The large group was easily accommodated as they were Sunday regulars to the restaurant. They ate and laughed, as Francisco regaled the group with stories of his days traveling all over the country, teaching capoeira seminars.

Mercedes even let it slip that she was in town for a burlesque performance, and she ended up inviting the group to the show that night.

Mercedes and Raul spent the rest of the day enjoying Times Square, and taking in the sights and sounds of the city. Shortly after six that evening, they headed back to the hotel, to allow Mercedes time to get ready for her show, and get to the club by eight that night. As Raul watched Mercedes perform her first set, he got the same feeling he had the night before.

Watching Mercedes dance to Eartha Kitt's "Careless Love" he wondered if the song had some underlying meaning for her. He could tell by the expression on her face that she felt the lyrics of the song and he thought maybe she had been hurt by love.

Perhaps some careless person from her past toyed with her heart and emotions, and that's why she was reluctant to get involved in a serious relationship. Raul knew that, for whatever reason, Mercedes had a fear of commitment. He could tell in the way she held back when he seemed to get too close. He could tell just by talking to some of her past partners.

The previous week he spent a few days talking to a couple of Mercedes' exes to see if they could possibly be behind whoever was stalking her. His team was still tracking down two of her most recent exes, but from what he was told by the others painted the picture of a woman who was into dating, but not for the long haul.

He planned on asking her about her exes, but not until they were back in Atlanta. For now, he was content looking at this beautiful woman on stage as she spun, dipped, and gyrated her hips to the music.

* * *

"I'LL BE BACK AROUND five or six. I have my cell phone on if you need anything," Raul told Mercedes as he came down the stairs, to leave for work. They had just returned from New York on an early morning flight, so he could make it into the office before ten a.m.

Mercedes' performance went well last night, and she was ready to unpack and do some redesigning on new costumes and even practice a new set. She was feeling good about the way the weekend went. She even thought that maybe Raul was overreacting to the whole stalker situation.

Mercedes wondered if the person who broke into her home wasn't just trying to scare her a little, for whatever reason, and now had moved on.

The trip to New York went off without a hitch. Maybe she could move back home and resume her regular schedule. She felt herself getting too attached to being around Raul. She had begun to feel particularly comfortable in his home.

And she knew that if they kept down this road, it could lead to developing serious feelings for this man. Something told her that with Raul it wouldn't just be sex. She couldn't let that happen. Not while she was living with the man.

He seemed to read too deeply into her inner thoughts as was.

"Great, I'm sure I won't need anything though," Mercedes responded. She looked him up and down. He wore a pair of dark blue slacks and a light blue, button-up shirt, with a pair of freshly polished black Stefano Bemer shoes.

Mercedes unconsciously bit her lower lip. It didn't matter what he wore, Raul always looked like he stepped off the runway. She bet he looked even better naked …

"I'm sure, but in the event you should need me, I'm a phone call away," Raul said, interrupting her fantasy.

She looked in his eyes and saw the knowing glint in them. With a few steps he closed the gap between them and pulled her into his arms. Before she could even protest, he swooped down and placed a lingering kiss good-bye on her lips.

She absentmindedly tilted her head to grant him better access to her mouth. The kiss was too brief, and before she could gain her bearings it ended.

Raul placed another kiss on her forehead and turned to head out the door.

"Don't forget to put in the alarm code once I leave," he reminded her.

Mercedes was brought back to reality as she heard the door close. She walked over to punch in the code, marveling at how his kiss had the ability to make time stop.

Reminiscing over the feel of his lips on hers, she shivered.

Yeah, it's definitely time to put some distance between us, she thought.

They hadn't even had sex yet, and she was already losing track of time and reality when he kissed her. Besides, maybe the whole stalker thing was over with. She hadn't received any new threats. No hang up calls to her knowledge, at least not on her cell phone. And in New York there hadn't been a trace of any threats.

She planned to talk to Raul about it later that night. She knew he probably wouldn't like her going back to her apartment, but it was her life and she wanted to get back to what she knew.

Maybe she could convince Raul to hire one of his men to check in on her at her own apartment. That way, she could have her distance and still be kept safe.

As she worked at designing her costumes, over the next few hours, Mercedes convinced herself more and more that going back home was the right thing to do. She thought about how she was going to break it to Raul that she was going back to her apartment.

Just when she believed she had a plan in place, her phone rang.

Looking at the number, she found it odd that this person would be calling her.

"Hi, Ron, how are you?" Mercedes asked, answering the phone. Ron Sherman was the principal at her school. Mercedes, along with two other assistant principals, worked closely with Ron to ensure the success of their school.

It was their summer break, and though they all worked well together, they rarely spoke to one another over the summer until a few weeks before the fall semester started. Most of the staff made plans to go away with family or just take time off to decompress from the busy school year.

The fact that Ron was calling Mercedes in the middle of July sent alarm bells off in her head.

"Hi, Mercedes. I'm sorry to interrupt your day. But I was wondering if you were in town and had time to meet me at the school today?"

Mercedes could hear in his voice that whatever this issue was, it was serious. She wondered if someone on their staff or one of their students had been hurt.

A few years ago, a student of theirs was killed in a car accident over the summer break, and Mercedes received a similar phone call.

"Sure, Ron. Is everything okay?" she asked, feeling her anxiety grow.

"Uh, well, everything is fine. We just need to talk to you."

"We?" Hearing it was more than just Ron who wanted to speak with her caused the hairs on the back of Mercedes' neck to stand up.

"Yes, myself and Superintendent Walters."

Mercedes stood. If the superintendent of schools was going to be there, it must be something serious.

"O-Okay. When did you want to meet?" She tried to keep her voice calm.

"We were hoping today. As soon as possible," Ron responded.

"I can be there in thirty minutes," Mercedes answered.

"Great, we will see you in thirty minutes," Ron said before hanging up the phone.

Mercedes didn't like the sound of this. She wondered if she was being terminated, and if so, for what reason.

She had an impeccable record as both a teacher and as an assistant principal. Mercedes had to admit that the job could be demanding. In fact, she'd had a couple of run-ins with new teachers, but nothing too serious. Besides, she never let differences get in the way of doing her job.

Mercedes went upstairs to change into a plum-colored business skirt and matching blazer. She was not sure what this meeting was about, but didn't want to show up looking unprofessional. She thought about calling Raul or leaving a message with his assistant, but decided against it.

She assumed she'd be back long before Raul got home.

He didn't have to know she ever left.

Once Mercedes arrived at the school, she was greeted by Ron's assistant, Marcy. Marcy told her Ron was still meeting with the superintendent, and that he'd be with her shortly. As she waited, Mercedes' nervousness grew. By now, she figured this wasn't something about one of their students or staff, but about her.

She went over and over in her head any possible complaints of misconduct or disagreements she had with parents or staff. She remembered none. There were a few minor disagreements of teaching style she had with members of the teaching staff, but nothing of major importance.

After about ten minutes of waiting, Ron's door opened, and he came out to meet Mercedes.

"Mercedes, thank you for coming down on such a short notice," he greeted her with a smile that didn't quite meet his eyes.

Mercedes wanted to ask if she really had a choice but held her tongue.

"Hi, Ron, it's no problem. Can you tell me what this is about?" she asked, not wanting to beat around the bush with small talk.

Ron nodded. "Why don't we step into my office? Superintendent Walters is here as well," Ron said, gesturing for Mercedes to follow him.

As she entered the room, she saw the superintendent sitting at the round, wooden table in the corner of Ron's office. When she rose, Mercedes moved to the table and greeted Superintendent Walters with a handshake. Mrs. Walters was about five inches shorter than Mercedes, but her professional attitude and demeanor gave her a commanding presence.

Superintendent Walters was a tough leader, but she had always been fair and commanded the best of her staff and her students. Mercedes could tell by the expression on Walters' face this meeting was not a friendly call.

"Please, have a seat, Ms. Holmes," Walters requested as she sat in her own seat.

Ron followed, pulling out a chair for himself. It wasn't until she sat down that Mercedes noticed an open laptop in the middle of the table, and an envelope sitting on the table next to it.

Superintendent Walters started. "Ms. Holmes, some disturbing information has come to our attention."

Mercedes raised an eyebrow but remained silent.

"A couple of days ago, Mr. Sherman and I received separate packages in the mail. They were DVDs of some recorded, uh, performances of yours." She said the word *performances* like the word tasted sour coming out of her mouth.

"I'm sorry, you said you received videotaped performances of me? What were these performances?"

Mercedes believed Walters was talking about her burlesque performances but didn't want to assume.

She remembered back to when Devyn had been blackmailed by her ex after he secretly recorded them having sex. She didn't want to believe someone was doing the same thing to her.

"They looked like they were taking place at some club, in front of an audience," Walters stated.

Mercedes almost sighed in relief. She was relieved to find out that this wasn't a sex tape, but then the realization that one of her burlesque performances had been mailed to her bosses left her stunned.

"Mr. Sherman and I received these DVDs on the same day. At first, we did not think much of it. We realize our staff has a life outside of this building, and you weren't doing anything illegal. However ..." Superintendent Walters paused and turned to Ron.

Mercedes felt her heart sink as she looked between Ron and Walters.

She knew she was not going to like what Walters said next.

"The following day," he continued, "we began getting calls and emails from some of our students' parents. It seems whoever sent this DVD to us, also sent it to a number of parents. Many of them were understandably upset."

Mercedes nearly slumped back in her chair. She felt like she'd just gotten the wind knocked out of her. Did someone really send the parents of her students a video of her burlesque performances?

Mercedes made it a point not to get too personal with the members of her staff. She never told anyone at her school she danced burlesque. Superintendent Walters was right, what each staff member did in their private life was just that, private. Mercedes was not ashamed of her performing, and never would be.

However, she recognized that not everyone was as progressive as she was, and that some people saw burlesque as a form of whoring oneself, for lack of a better term. Mercedes was raised in the type of environment where her performing would be looked down on.

"Is that the DVD?" Mercedes asked, motioning toward the DVD case that sat next to the laptop.

"Yes, it is," Walters said, nodding her head.

"Can I see it?" Mercedes noticed Ron look questioningly at Walters, before she nodded her head in agreement. Ron slid the laptop closer to him and placed the DVD to play it.

Within seconds, Mercedes saw herself on stage at The Black Kitty dancing to Nina Simone's "Feeling Good" as she danced and stripped down to her revealing thong and pasties.

Out of the corner of her eye, Mercedes saw Ron avert his eyes from the screen and clear his throat before turning off the DVD.

"This note was also attached to the copy that was sent to the parents," Ron said, sliding over a folded, white piece of paper.

The note read: *Is this who you want teaching your children?*

Mercedes closed her eyes as all of this sank in. Whoever was stalking her definitely had not given up. They were now targeting her career.

Mercedes felt the need to defend herself.

"This is ridiculous. Whoever sent these letters is violating my privacy," she said, struggling to keep her voice even.

"Well, technically, Ms. Holmes, you're performing for the public so no privacy violation was committed," Walters reminded Mercedes.

"Yes, but sending these videos to the parents? That has to be some kind of violation of privacy. As you stated, Superintendent Walters, what staff does in our private time should not be called into question as long as it's not illegal. I have never done anything against the law, and I certainly never brought anything to do with my performing into my professional career."

Mercedes was barely keeping her rising anger in check.

"Ms. Holmes, that is our school's policy, but now that this has been brought to the attention of the parents of our school, we have to look further into this. A number of parents are upset about what they saw. And—"

Walters held up her hand to stop Mercedes who opened her mouth to defend herself. "And I agree with you, nothing on this tape is illegal, but there is a matter of ethics. Some parents are questioning if someone who strips on the side can be a good role model for their children."

Walters' last comment made Mercedes see red.

"Burlesque is *not* stripping, and though I personally do not believe there is anything wrong with strippers or stripping, I must inform you that burlesque has a long history of performance in this country and many others. It is a legitimate art form."

Mercedes was pissed.

She was angered that whoever was stalking her would target her career like this, and she was angered at the way Walters' was looking down her nose at burlesque performers.

"Ms. Holmes, I understand you're upset, but you must understand our position. Parents are contacting us asking if we are teaching their children to strip in class. I know that sounds preposterous to you, but until we do a full investigation and make sure no codes of conduct were violated, we're going to place you on administrative leave."

Mercedes was confused. Administrative leave? They were in the middle of summer. There weren't any classes going on. What exactly would this administrative leave entail?

"So, what does this mean?" she asked, looking Superintendent Walters directly in the eye.

"Mercedes," Ron interjected, "we'll have to review with our legal team to make sure your dancing does not violate the ethical clause in your contract, and then we will meet with the board of directors to see what they want to do.

"We are also meeting with the parents who've shown concern over the DVD," he finished.

"How long will that take?" Mercedes asked, looking between them.

Superintendent Walters spoke up this time, "Well some members of the board are on vacation, and I am going away next week for two weeks—"

"So this could take all the way up to the fall semester, possibly longer?" Mercedes asked, cutting Walters off.

Ron quickly interjected, "We will try to get this over and done with as soon as possible. Mercedes, you know you are one of our most prized employees."

Mercedes looked at Ron. He appeared sincere, but she knew this was over his head.

"Could I lose my job over this?" Mercedes asked Superintendent Walters.

Walters avoided eye contact, and Mercedes had her answer.

"We are hoping it does not come to that," Walters responded.

Mercedes sat through the rest of the meeting in a daze. She was livid, but felt powerless because she had no idea who could be behind this. It'd been two weeks and they were still no closer to finding out who could be stalking her. Mercedes felt as if she were having some sort of out-of-body experience as she watched Superintendent Walters' lips move.

Mercedes was too busy trying to piece together when this stalker had time to record her and send the DVDs out. There was no time-stamp on the tape, but Mercedes remembered she last performed that set back in May. From the angle of the tape, it looked as if the person was standing somewhere in the back audience.

That narrowed the list down to hundreds of people. Anyone could buy a ticket to a performance and have a seat in the audience. While cameras and filming weren't allowed in The Black Kitty, it wouldn't be too difficult to sneak a camera in and film a performance. Mercedes tried to focus on what Superintendent Walters and Ron were saying, but her brain was too clogged with the different possibilities.

Whoever this was had access to her in a place she had come to feel the safest. The Black Kitty had become a sanctuary to her, of sorts, and now she felt violated.

First her home and now this.

When the meeting finally ended, Ron promised he would keep in touch and update Mercedes on everything that was going on. Mercedes mumbled a response to Ron, shook hands with the superintendent, and hurried to her car.

Once in her car, Mercedes didn't know what to do. She wanted to call Devyn and vent to her but Devyn was in South America with her husband and children. She didn't want to interrupt her vacation. Mercedes thought about going back to Raul's place, but did not want to be alone.

She felt open and exposed and vulnerable, which was a feeling she worked hard never to feel. Part of the reason she'd started burlesque so long ago was to overcome her fear of being exposed or vulnerable, by facing what most people deemed their greatest fear—being naked in front of an audience.

Mercedes believed that if she could let go of that fear, she wouldn't feel so weak when it came to emotions and relationships. But now, here she was feeling vulnerable and, admittedly, a little fearful. Whoever this was knew her movements, when she was out of town, and when she performed. Mercedes couldn't believe that just that morning she started to think this nightmare was over and that whoever this was had forgotten about her.

It seemed she was not so lucky. Mercedes contemplated what to do next. Devyn was away, Raul was working, and most of her other friends were either out of town or at work. It was the middle of the day, and she didn't know where to go.

The decision was made for her when her phone began ringing.

"Mercedes, where are you?" Raul's voice blasted through her car speakers. She heard an odd note she'd never heard in Raul's voice before.

He seemed worried. Or maybe afraid?

"I, uh, I'm in my car right now," she responded, feeling a little apprehensive to tell him she'd left the house without informing him.

"In your car where?" Raul demanded.

Mercedes sighed. She knew he was not going to like her response. "I had a meeting with my school principal and superintendent."

She stopped short of telling him what the meeting was about.

"School's out for the summer. What was your meeting about?"

Mercedes found herself perturbed that he would question her about her whereabouts … she was a grown woman, not some invalid who needed to be taken care of twenty-four seven.

She was already angry after what happened in the meeting she'd just been in, and now Raul's tone was making her feel even more irritated.

"So … what, I can't even go to my job without having to check-in with you? Is that what you're saying?" As soon as the words left her mouth, she felt a pang of guilt.

Raul had unselfishly opened up his home to her to keep her safe, and now she was acting like an adolescent who couldn't get her way.

"That's exactly what the hell I'm saying. Or have you forgotten there is someone out there who means to do real harm to you?"

Mercedes sighed. "I haven't forgotten. I couldn't even if I wanted to," she said dejectedly.

"What happened?" he asked as if he knew the reason she'd been summoned to her school had something to do with her stalker. Maybe he could hear it in her voice. He had a way of reading her that unnerved and comforted her at the same time.

She sighed. "My principal, superintendent, and some parents were sent a video of one of my performances. I was placed on administrative leave."

As the words fell from her lips, Mercedes felt her anger begin to rise again.

"Come to my office. Now," he told her, his tone leaving no room for her to argue.

Mercedes wanted to hate the way her nipples budded at the deep command in his voice. She shouldn't be turned on by his borderline barbarian act, but damn it if she wasn't.

"I'm about twenty minutes away from your office," Mercedes told him.

"I know. Get here in fifteen," he said before hanging up.

Mercedes sat stunned, for the second time that day.

He knew? How could he possibly know how far she was from his office? And who the hell was he ordering to get there in fifteen minutes?

She tried to recall if she'd put his address in, but remembered that Raul had driven her car when they picked it up from the dealer after her tires were fixed. She assumed he input his office address in her GPS, and possibly a tracker, which was how he knew where she was.

A small part of her felt safer just knowing he was keeping track of her, but she would definitely ask him about it. Twenty-five minutes later, Mercedes was pulling up into the parking lot of the building that housed Raul's offices. He was already outside waiting for her.

She pulled into the closest parking space, and before she could even finish turning the ignition off, he was opening her car door.

"Are you all right?" he asked, staring intently into her eyes, trying to discern her mood. He gripped both of her arms.

Mercedes nodded. "Yes, I'm fine."

Raul stared at her for another heartbeat, as if he thought she wasn't being completely forthcoming.

"Come with me," he said as he closed her car door. He placed his hand at the small of her back and quickly strode to the elevators that would take them to his office.

The anger that Mercedes felt when he demanded she get to his office dissipated when she saw the worry in his eyes.

Once they made it to his office, Raul pulled Mercedes down the hall, past his assistant's desk. Mercedes was barely given time to say a quick hello to the older woman, before she found herself in what she presumed was Raul's office. His large, corner office was decorated in dark, earthy colors, with a few plants placed around the room, which gave it an inviting feel.

There was a large, cherry wood desk in the center of the room, and a dark leather couch off to the side, at the back of the office. Mercedes heard a *click* as the office door closed.

For some reason this small sound, instead of a loud slam, caused Mercedes even more worry. She knew Raul was angry at her for leaving and not telling him.

"Tell me what happened," he said gruffly once she was seated.

"Well, hello to you, too," she said in defiance. He wasn't the only one who could be angry. Hell, she was the one who had just been placed on administrative leave.

Raul leaned against this desk and crossed his legs at the ankles in front of him as he waited for Mercedes to explain.

"Tell me what happened," he ordered again.

She felt like a child being scolded, which she hated. To place them on equal footing, she stood and took a few steps back to give herself some breathing room. The intensity of his gaze on her made her feel the need to put some distance between them.

"I got a call from the principal of my school, Ron Sherman, a couple hours after you left," she finally began. "He said he needed to see me as soon as possible. He didn't tell me what the issue was. The superintendent of schools was there also." Mercedes paused to catch her breath.

She glanced at Raul and saw she held his full attention. The way he was looking at her rattled her for many reasons.

"They told me that they'd been sent a video of me. It was a video of one of my performances at The Black Kitty."

She saw Raul's gaze grow even more intense.

"The video had also been sent to parents at the school. Some complained, and now they're doing an investigation of me to see if my dancing violates any code of ethics. I'm on administrative leave until further notice." She stopped, taking in a deep breath.

"Mierda!" Raul slammed his palm onto his desk. Drawing himself up to his full height, Raul approached Mercedes. "And you weren't going to say anything about this to me?"

"It just happened right before you called. I was going to tell you," she defended.

"You were going to tell me? And when was that? Next week? Next month? Let's get something straight. I am the first phone call you make when shit like this happens. I am the one you call first … no, scratch that, I'm who you call *before* you leave the house. I'm not playing games. This isn't a joke. Someone is out there and they mean to do you real harm.

"Do you have a copy of the video?" he asked, his tone sharp.

Mercedes could do nothing but nod in response to his question.

Raul stuck out his hand. "Let me have it. I can have it analyzed to help us figure out whoever is behind this."

Mercedes pulled the copy of the DVD that was sent to Ron from out of her purse and handed it to him.

"Was this all that was sent?" he asked.

"No, there was also a note," she said, pulling out the note that had been sent with the video.

Raul examined the note, and Mercedes could see his nostrils slightly flare.

He was angry.

"Who else has touched this?"

"I'm not sure. Me, Ron, my superintendent. Aside from that I don't know. Why?" she asked quietly, still reeling from being chastised by him.

"I want to have it dusted for fingerprints. It's unlikely, but whoever sent it may have slipped up and touched it with their bare hands … although it's a long shot.

"Whoever's behind this was methodical enough to record you undetected, get personal information on your employers and parents at your school. They are surely intelligent enough to wear gloves when handling the letter or DVD. Still, it won't hurt to dust for fingerprints.

"Since you work with children, your principal's and superintendent's fingerprints are already in the FBI's database. So, we can weed yours out from there, and if we find anyone else's, maybe we can match them in our system."

Mercedes nodded. She understood that whoever was doing this was probably cautious enough not to leave fingerprints behind. She sighed in frustration.

At hearing her sigh, Raul's gaze on her softened.

Raul had been pissed hearing she went out and didn't even think of calling him. He was slowly realizing part of his emotion was more fear than anger. He was afraid of something happening to her. Mercedes was beginning to mean a lot to him in such a short period of time.

Raul called Lorenzo to take both the DVD and letter for fingerprint analysis. He then turned the chair Mercedes had been sitting in and gestured for her to sit down.

"Now, let's talk about you leaving the house without my knowledge."

Mercedes' eyebrows shot up at the recrimination in his voice. "I already told you I thought I was just going for a short meeting. I didn't think whoever was stalking me was behind this. I—"

"No, you didn't think, because for some reason you thought this person up and decided to leave you alone. The same reason you were thinking it was safe to go back to your apartment and get back to your normal routine, right?"

Mercedes looked shocked at the accuracy of his words. She had been thinking of a way to tell him just that before she got the phone call from Ron.

How did he know what she was thinking?

"Don't look so surprised. I could tell this morning what you were thinking. You were distancing yourself from me."

Mercedes couldn't deny his words. She had been more quiet and contemplative on their plane ride back to Atlanta. She could admit to herself that it wasn't only about thinking the stalker had left her alone, but her growing closeness with Raul.

The past weekend in New York, and the two weeks she spent living in his home, showed him to be much more than the hot, Brazilian playboy she pegged him for. Not only was he a badass security expert with a ripped body, but he was kind and compassionate, and she sometimes felt he could look right down into her soul.

That unsettled her as much as the knowledge someone was out there trying to sabotage her life.

But instead of revealing any of this to Raul, Mercedes clammed up. Again, she folded her arms across her chest, as if counseling her true emotions.

Raul recognized the stance for what it was. He refused to let her off the hook that easily.

He took a few steps closer until they were now face-to-face. "You're running because you feel the same thing I do. Your feelings for me are growing stronger and it makes you uncomfortable. You think putting distance between us will help, but that's not going to happen for two reasons.

"Do you know what those reasons are?" he asked, looking her directly in the eye and raising an eyebrow.

Mercedes was overwhelmed by his closeness and the challenge she saw in his eyes. She opened her mouth to speak, but nothing came out. Clamping her mouth shut, she merely shook her head in response to his question.

He waved his hand back and forth between them. "For one, this has been here all along. Since the first time we met. It's not going away. And two, I won't let anyone, not even you, compromise your safety. There is someone out there who is intent on harming you. I'm not about to let that happen, so get this silly bullshit idea of you moving out of my place and back to your apartment out of your head."

By the time Raul finished speaking, Mercedes felt herself both turned on and frightened. Turned on because Raul was undeniably sexy when he got all protective and possessive like this.

And afraid at once again realizing he was right. Whoever this was behind her stalking wasn't going away quietly. She dropped her arms to her side, no longer defensive. Maybe she could give in to whatever this was between them. It didn't mean she would fall in love, right?

Giving into the chemistry between her and Raul didn't mean she had to lose herself. Mercedes had been in plenty of relationships before.

She may have even loved a few of her exes ... not been in love, mind you, but loved them as people. She could handle whatever this was with Raul. Mercedes lifted her gaze to meet Raul's.

"Okay," she said, nodding her head. "You're right, I'm not going anywhere."

Before the words were fully out of her mouth, Raul pulled her in for a scorching kiss. When his tongue slid across the seam of her lips, urging them apart, Mercedes complied. She moaned as his tongue snaked around hers, tasting every inch of her mouth.

Mercedes' hands moved up Raul's strong chest and wrapped them around his neck, pulling him in even deeper. She was lost in the feel of his lips moving over hers and his hands as they reached around to grip her behind. His growing length pressed against her stomach.

Wetness pooled between her legs.

Mercedes couldn't even remember why she had been tempted to run from him in the first place. His kiss had the power to make her temporarily forget her fear of commitment and love. All that mattered right now was this feeling.

Unfortunately, their intimate moment was cut short by a knock on the door.

Raul was the first to pull away from the embrace. Mercedes saw the passion in his eyes and shivered. He placed a quick peck on her cheek.

"This isn't over," he promised in her ear.

"I'm counting on it," she retorted.

This got Raul's attention, and the embers of passion in his eyes grew even more. Before he could respond, there was another knock on the door, this one a little more forceful. Raul growled under his breath.

"Come in," he yelled through the door, as Mercedes made her way to the couch in the corner of his office.

"Hey, boss, it looks like you were right. The only fingerprints on the letter are from Mercedes, Ron Sherman, and the superintendent," Lorenzo stated, handing Raul the fingerprint report.

"I thought so, but do me a favor and do a full report on Sherman and the superintendent," Raul instructed.

"Already started it, boss." Lorenzo was one of Raul's top men. He'd known that Raul would want to have anyone who came in contact with these letters investigated.

But hearing this threw Mercedes off.

"You think Ron or my superintendent could have something to do with this?" she asked, standing.

Raul motioned for Lorenzo to leave before he turned to Mercedes.

"It's a precaution, but I've had cases where stalkers sometimes send themselves letters or threats to throw us off the investigation. They try to make themselves look like a victim or innocent bystander instead of the culprit. We're just checking all possibilities," he told her reassuringly.

Mercedes nodded. That made sense, and he had a lot more experience with this type of thing than she did. Not for the first time, Mercedes wanted to ask Raul what it was that had gotten him into this type of work.

She knew about his military background, but with a background like his, he could've gone into any field. His father owned an extremely successful bank in his homeland of Brazil. Then what caused a man like Raul to go into security instead of finance like his father and his best friend?

As much as she wanted to ask, Mercedes held back. Instead, she tried to focus on not letting her mind get too involved in the man who was protecting her.

Mercedes spent the rest of the day in Raul's office, where he ordered takeout, and together they went over a few more leads. The investigation of her apartment break-in brought up no suspects. The police couldn't find any foreign fingerprints. Even Raul's men had gone in to sweep the apartment after the police and they came up with nothing new.

Mercedes' had opened a PO box to have her mail forwarded to, so she wouldn't have to worry about going back to get her mail. Raul had one of his employees pick up her mail a couple times a week and bring it to the office so he could deliver it to her.

He was grateful for this foresight.

Raul hadn't told Mercedes, but her stalker had sent a number of threatening letters. All of them on plain, white paper, the same as the note that'd been attached to the sent DVDs.

The letters were vile in nature, and he didn't want to expose her to them. He'd had his team catalog and collect any evidence they could get from these letters, but so far they hadn't come up with anything.

A few hours later, they left Raul's office. Mercedes peered through her rearview mirror to see Raul's car following her as they drove back to his home that evening and she knew something had changed.

Her hands gripped the steering wheel firmly as her body grew heated at the thoughts of her and Raul tangled in his sheets. She wasn't about to fall in love with the man, but she damn sure wanted more from him than just his protection.

CHAPTER 11

ercedes smiled at the name displayed on her cell phone screen. "Hey, Mal. How are you doing?"

It was Friday evening, and she was beginning to get ready for her performance at The Black Kitty that night.

She was feeling antsy seeing as this was her first time back there since she found out she had been recorded. She was grateful for the distraction.

"Hey, sis. Just chillin'. Wanted to call on my way home from work. It's been a minute since we last talked."

The truth was, it had only been a week since Mercedes last talked to her brother, but that was a long time for them. They usually spoke at least twice a week. Mercedes appreciated the close relationship she had with her brother.

Despite being raised by different standards of freedom, they'd forged a close relationship. Jamal often intervened when he felt their father was going too overboard in how he spoke to Mercedes. He was never confrontational, but would try to divert their father's attention to give Mercedes a little breathing room. She was thankful to have Jamal on her side.

However, there were still things she kept from him, like her performing and the fact that she dated men and women. At times, she felt guilty about keeping these aspects of her life from her brother.

"Yeah, it has been. I'm sorry, it's been a busy week," Mercedes said by way of explanation.

It hadn't been that busy, but Mercedes found herself spending more and more time with Raul in the evenings after he came home from work. They would often spend hours watching the latest season of *Orange is the New Black* on Netflix, playing board games, or just talking.

A smile spread across Mercedes' face as she remembered the kisses Raul would steal, catching her off guard as they watched TV or sat outside on his back patio. They hadn't gone as far as that night in New York, but Mercedes knew that would soon change.

"No doubt. My week's been a little crazy, too, but I have some time off coming up. I was thinking of coming to A-t-l for a visit," he said, using Atlanta's nickname.

"Um," Mercedes said nervously. She hadn't told Jamal or her parents about being stalked or living with Raul.

Jamal picked up on her hesitation.

"Um? Dang, Cedes, if you didn't want me to visit just say so," he said jokingly, but Mercedes could hear his underlying hurt.

"Shut up, you know it's not that," she scoffed, trying to lighten the mood. "I love when you come to visit. It's just that, I'm not staying at my apartment for now, and I don't know when I'll be back."

"Where are you staying? Is everything all right?"

Mercedes could hear the worry in her brother's voice. She didn't like the idea of keeping more secrets between them. She decided to let him in on what was going on, but with one condition.

"Well, everything is all right so far, but there's something I need to tell you … but you have to promise to keep it to yourself and not tell Mom or Dad," she hedged.

"Cedes, what is it? You're sounding a little scary now."

Mercedes sighed. "Someone has been stalking me."

"What? Have you been hurt? What's going on?" he demanded to know.

"I'm okay. It's a little bit of a long story."

Mercedes proceeded to tell her brother about the hang up phone calls and the break-in into her apartment. She told him this person contacted her employers and told them some lies, instead of the full truth since it would expose her burlesque dancing.

She still wanted to keep that secret from her brother until she was comfortable.

Jamal was understandably upset with her for not telling him until now. He was concerned for her safety, even after she told him she was staying with Raul while he helped figure out whoever was behind this.

He insisted on coming to visit her in a few weeks when he could get some time off from his job. Mercedes didn't object.

She knew if the roles were reversed she'd be worried about his safety, too. After fifteen minutes of trying to reassure her brother that she was fine and convincing him not to tell their parents, she hung up and began gathering her costume for her performance that night. The antsy feeling she had earlier returned.

Raul's face dropped as soon as she came down the stairs.

"What's wrong?" He pulled her into an embrace.

"I just spoke with my brother. I told him everything … well, almost everything."

Raul pulled back and gave her a questioning look at her cryptic statement.

"My family doesn't know I do burlesque," she answered.

"Why not?"

Sighing, she ran a hand over her hair. Mercedes debated how much she wanted to tell Raul about her family.

"I grew up in a strict Christian household. My father is a preacher, and his thoughts on women are … let's just say they're antiquated. He still hasn't forgiven me fully for going away for college or moving to Atlanta afterwards. He certainly wouldn't approve of me performing," she answered, putting it diplomatically.

She knew her father would flip the hell out if he knew she danced and took her clothes off in front of an audience. She looked up at Raul and could tell he wanted to ask more, but thankfully he held his questions.

Right now she just wanted to focus on getting through tonight's performance.

"Let's eat before you have to get ready to go." He escorted her to the back entrance that led to the patio.

Raul had fixed a delicious salad with Brazilian rice and beans and corn tortillas. Mercedes ate it up, thoroughly enjoying his culinary skills.

It was a simple meal but delicious nonetheless.

About halfway through their dinner, Raul announced, "I spoke with Quince today."

Mercedes looked over at him. Quince was an old boyfriend. She knew Raul was going to interview her most recent exes, so this news shouldn't have surprised her, but she squirmed in her chair.

"Oh yeah, did you find out anything interesting?"

Raul shrugged. "Nothing too interesting. He's still in Atlanta, just had been away on business for a few weeks, which is why it took us a while to track him down.

"He seemed a little miffed over being dumped, but not enough to be your stalker. Still, I'll have my team keep an eye on him."

"Thank y—"

"Stop thanking me." Raul shot her with a stern look.

Mercedes smiled.

"Anyway, like I said he still seemed upset that you dumped him. Why did you break up with him?"

Mercedes stopped dating Quince close to two years ago. They'd been together for all of a few months. She knew his ego was more bruised at being dumped than any real emotional investment.

Mercedes rolled her eyes as she placed her glass on the table. "He was more attracted to my sexuality than me." She shrugged.

Raul tilted his head. "What does that mean?"

"It means that when he heard I dated both men and women he thought it meant threesomes and orgies where he was the only man involved."

Raul raised an eyebrow. "And that wasn't the case?"

Mercedes had dated a lot of people in her youth, and had even indulged in a few threesomes, but that was years ago. When she first moved out of her parents' house, she was the typical good girl gone bad, for a little while.

She'd done and experimented a lot in her youth, but that wasn't her style anymore. She still dated who she found attractive, but she was not into sharing partners or random hookups anymore.

Mercedes looked Raul square in the eye. "No. That's not my style. I like men and women, but that doesn't mean I spread my legs for just anyone. I don't like sharing either."

"Wait, is that why you were so mad that night after Nikola and Devyn's wedding? You believed I set you up to have a threesome with Cindy?" he asked.

"Yeah, you wouldn't be the first guy to try it," she admitted.

"Querida, that's not my style. I don't have to sneak. If I want something, I'm upfront."

Mercedes nodded, recognizing he was telling the truth. "I know that now, but I didn't know you then."

"That's fair. So, do you consider yourself bisexual?" he inquired at the same time he rose from his chair.

Mercedes lifted a shoulder in a shrug. "I don't really label it. I just like what I like."

"And what about me? Do you like me?" He pulled her from her chair, into his body.

"You already know the answer to that," she said, as she allowed herself to be taken into his arms.

Raul smiled that sexy grin of his. "I want to hear you say it."

Mercedes found herself staring at his lips. She licked her own. "I like you, Raul."

Raul sat, tugging her onto his lap, so she was straddling him. He pulled her lips down to meet his. He nibbled at her lips before completely devouring her mouth.

The usual heady sensations that happened whenever their lips met overtook Mercedes. She felt his hands glide up and down her back, making contact with exposed skin as they found their way to her uncovered shoulders.

Raul deftly loosened the string of Mercedes' halter top dress, letting it fall to expose her perky breasts.

"You have such beautiful breasts. I've wanted to devour them since the first time I saw you on stage," he said, inching back to stare at them.

In all honesty, Raul had wanted to see all of her since the first time they met, but seeing her on stage, performing nearly naked increased his hunger for her. He had to remind himself over and over that his first job was to keep her safe while she performed. Not get sidetracked with his own desire to feel her writhing beneath him.

But right then it was a different story.

Mercedes wasn't performing. She was safe in his arms, and her eyes were filled with a need he knew was a reflection of his own. Raul lowered his head and licked, first one, then a second pert nipple. Mercedes moaned at the contact and arched her back, thrusting her breasts in his face even more, encouraging him.

Raul was happy to oblige.

He latched on to her left breast and suckled, while he let his hand massage and play with the other nipple. He alternated between both breasts, giving each side his full attention. Mercedes grasped onto Raul's shoulders as the delightful sensations of his mouth on her rushed through her body.

She reflexively began to rock her hips back and forth on his lap, trying to ease the ache that began to develop between her lips. She felt Raul's growing bulge against her stomach. This spurred them both on.

Raul continued feasting on her breasts, while his fingers eased up her thighs and found the edge of her panties.

Mercedes aided him by spreading her legs, making room for his fingers. Mercedes' fingernails dug into Raul's sleeves when his two fingers entered her wetness. She ground her hips on his fingers as Raul lifted his head from her breasts, pulling her head down for another kiss. She moaned loudly into his mouth. She bucked and rode his fingers, and when his thumb came up to massage her clit, her release was imminent.

Moving his head to suckle on the skin behind her ear, Raul allowed his fingers to quicken. Coming, Mercedes threw her head back. She rode his fingers through her orgasm, panting loudly.

Raul pulled his fingers from Mercedes wet channel and licked them clean. He groaned. "You taste so fucking good."

Mercedes' body felt like it was on fire. As if the orgasm she'd just had never happened. She needed him to relieve the ache in her belly. They both needed it. But as Raul prepared to move this encounter to his bedroom, Mercedes' phone beeped.

Jarred by the noise, they pulled apart. It took both a second to realize what that noise was, until Mercedes finally remembered.

"Th-That's my alarm. We're going to be late." Mercedes had set her phone alarm to remind her of her scheduled performances.

"Mierda!" Raul cursed in Brazilian, as he shifted himself in his pants, and eased Mercedes off his lap.

She grinned at his reaction. She didn't want to leave either, but she had to.

"We're not finished with this conversation," Raul said to her. By the way he said the word "conversation" she knew talking was not what he was referring to.

"You've said that before," she teased and stood up.

Raul took one look at the smirk on her swollen lips, and pulled her back down onto his lap. "Querida, I suggest you stop teasing me or the only stage you'll be performing on tonight is in my bedroom."

Mercedes' breath caught. She had no response as he used his finger to trace her jawline, his eyes boring into her own. But just as quickly as he pulled her down, he placed a short kiss on her lips and eased her up as he stood.

"Go get your things. I'll put the dishes away so we can head out." Raul quickly turned to pick up their plates and glasses.

Mercedes hurried up to her room to get her belongings and the costume she'd be wearing that night. She had a feeling that performing at The Black Kitty wasn't the only action she was going to have by night's end.

* * *

RAUL WATCHED as the woman on stage gracefully lifted her leg into the air as she leapt across. The woman he had come to know as Jazmine was a regular performer at The Black Kitty. She started her routine wearing a white feathered leotard, but she was now down to her white leggings, pasties, and en pointe shoes.

He could tell she had a great deal of ballet training, and that she mixed it with a more modern dance style.

She was around the same height as Mercedes, and had the physique of a dancer, with smooth skin the color of cocoa. By all accounts she was beautiful, but the woman that held his rapt attention was the one standing next to him.

Out of the corner of his eye, he could see flashes of emerald, blue, and purple, as Mercedes fluffed her peacock costume.

She was to hit the stage next, after Jazmine. Her closeness sent his senses into overdrive. Earlier in the evening, he'd come close to dragging her up to his bedroom and not letting her up for air until the next morning. If it wasn't for the damned alarm, they'd be in his bed, arms and legs entangled.

Now, he was here on full alert, with a few of his men positioned around the club to help keep her safe. Her stalker had videotaped her in this very club without anyone's knowledge.

They could be here tonight, watching her. Raul wouldn't blame her if she chose not to perform, but Mercedes wouldn't hear of it.

She was a trooper.

Once she realized this person's goal was to completely upend her life, Mercedes made the decision to live her life as normal as possible … within reason, of course. Raul respected that, and he was going to make damn sure whoever this was didn't have a chance to hurt Mercedes more than they already had.

Finally, Jazmine's set ended, and she came bounding down the stairs off the stage, and pressed a quick kiss to Mercedes' cheek, wishing her luck on her performance.

Just as quickly as she came down the stairs, Jazmine was gone, strutting down the hallway toward the locker room. Raul saw the woman who was tasked with collecting the performer's discarded costumes, gathering pieces of Jazmine's costume in her arms, before she hurried down the hallway as well.

The owner of the club, Mistress Coco, made her way to the stage, cheering the crowd to applaud one last time for Jazmine and beginning her introduction for Mercedes.

Coco's voice reverberated through the club. "Ladies, hold onto your wigs. And, fellas, hold on to your jockstraps!"

Raul smiled and turned to Mercedes. "She's one of a kind," he said, referring to Mistress Coco.

Mercedes laughed. "And she doesn't take lip from anyone."

"Remember, I'll be right here a few feet away and I have my men strategically placed around the club. You just focus on performing your little heart out," he said, reminding her of the safety precautions they'd taken.

Mercedes nodded. "I can do that."

She started up the stairs as Mistress Coco's introduction wound down, and the lights went low. Raul heard Etta James' voice wash over the crowd as she sang the opening chords to "Something's Got a Hold on Me".

Raul admitted to himself he could relate to the words of the song. While he wasn't ready to say it was love, he had feelings for Mercedes … feelings he'd never had for another woman. His mother's words about needing a wife floated back into his mind.

He shook his head and refocused on the task at hand. Choosing to ignore the questions in his head, he carefully watch the crowd and onlookers for any sudden movements, possible weapons, or even the flicker of a camera or video light.

He saw his men in the front and back of the audience and they were on high alert. He nodded when one of them made eye contact. Raul breathed a little easier knowing his men were on the job. After scanning the audience for a few moments, he returned his attention back to the stage and his stomach muscles instantly tightened.

Mercedes was now down to her heels, tights, and costume bra, with very little else, as she laid on her back on the stage floor, feet planted, knees bent, and thrusting her hips and swiveling them in the air.

Raul's body tightened. A surge of energy pulsed through his veins at hearing the claps and whistles from the men in the audience. A wave of jealousy that had him picturing himself snapping the neck of any man that got too close to her overtook him.

When he turned back to the stage, a small groan escaped his throat. What he wouldn't give to have her in that exact position, fully naked in his bed. He had every intention of making that happen sooner rather than later.

But before he could let his fantasy fully form in his mind, a quick movement out of the corner of his eye drew his attention. He saw his man, Lorenzo, who was closest to the stage, jump up in pursuit of a guy who was seated. The man appeared as if he was headed for the stage.

Raul didn't think twice before he was on stage, rushing to Mercedes, pulling her up and off the stage. Mercedes, shocked at his abrupt appearance, almost looked as if she was going to pull away, but she swiftly realized it was Raul and let him lead her off stage.

Without even looking back, Raul ushered Mercedes off the stage, down the stairs, and down the hall to the private changing room he'd requested for her. He knew his men had grabbed whoever it was that rushed the stage.

His primary concern was getting Mercedes out of harm's way and away from onlookers.

"What the hell was that?" Mercedes blurted out as they burst into the changing room, Raul shutting the door behind them.

He hurriedly checked the room to make sure no one was hiding inside, before turning to answer her question.

"Someone rushed the stage. Could just be an overanxious fan, but could be our guy. I'm going to find out." Just as Raul finished his statement, there were two light taps and then two heavy taps on the door. That was his team's signal.

Opening the door, he found himself face-to-face with Lorenzo.

"You got him?" Raul asked.

"Yeah, boss. Johnny's holding him. He doesn't have anything on him," Lorenzo answered.

"Wait here. No one comes in or out of this room," Raul instructed.

Mercedes looked too shocked to speak. He wanted to envelop her in his arms and assure her it was okay, but he had work to do. The sooner he spoke to this man the sooner he could get her out of here.

"Sure thing, boss," Lorenzo complied as Raul stepped out of the door, closing it behind him. Lorenzo stood on guard outside of the door while Raul went in search of Johnny. He met Mistress Coco in the hallway.

"They took him to my office. Down the hall to the right. And if that's the bastard who's trying to scare my Black Dahlia just let me have five minutes alone with him!" she told Raul tersely.

Even though the woman was a mere five foot three and in her sixties, Raul didn't doubt that she could easily hurt someone.

"Will do, ma'am, but you have to promise to leave something for me to handle when you're done," Raul said, meaning every word.

"I make no such promises," Mistress Coco said before turning and heading in the opposite direction.

Despite the possible danger, Raul smiled at the older woman's gumption. Raul made it to Mistress Coco's office and opened the door to see Johnny peering over the audience member who rushed the stage. The man was no taller than five six or five seven, with a medium build, and in his mid-to-late twenties.

With Johnny peering over him like he wanted to haul him outside behind the dumpsters, the man seemed to slink down in his seat.

"Name," Raul demanded.

The man barely made eye contact with Raul.

"You heard him. What's your fucking name?" Johnny repeated.

"Michael," he said in a low but even voice.

"Michael, why did you rush the stage like that?" Raul asked, stepping closer.

Michael shrugged his response. "I don't know."

Raul was working with a short fuse. Apparently sensing Raul's temper rise, Johnny stepped back as Raul hauled the man out of his chair and shoved him into the nearest wall.

"I'm sure you have no clue who the fuck you're playing with, but I'm telling you right fucking now, I'm not the one to be toyed with. As of right now, the only thing keeping me from slamming my fist into your face is that you have information I need. You've got until I count to three to spill it, or I'm wiping this fucking office floor with your face."

And with that, Raul let the man go and stepped back. When the man remained silent, it was as if he thought Raul was bluffing … until he started counting.

"One."

Raul removed his black blazer, unbuttoned the top button of his shirt, and neatly rolled up his sleeves. The man looked nervously between Johnny and Raul, but still remained quiet.

"Two."

Raul pulled his Glock 19 from its back holster, checked the chamber, and handed it to Johnny while giving Michael a deadly stare.

Michael swallowed at the smile that spread across Johnny's face.

"Thr—"

"Okay, okay. I was paid to do it," Michael blurted out before Raul could finish his countdown.

"By who?" Raul asked, not missing a beat.

"I don't know."

When he saw Raul take a threatening step forward, he held his hands up in front of his body. "No, seriously, I don't know!

"All I know is I got a message from an online dating website I created a profile on. The person asked me to come to this show tonight, and wait for Black Dahlia to perform. They told me to rush the stage, toss a bag of feathers on her, and call her a whore or something. That's it. I was never going to hurt her."

Raul glanced down at the pillowcase full of fake feathers the man had with him. Lorenzo retrieved the pillowcase from the man before he could throw them all over Mercedes.

Raul heard enough. He pushed Michael into the wall. "You call running up on stage and pulling a bullshit stunt like this *not hurting them*? How much did they pay you?"

"Two-hundred bucks. I'm sorry, I didn't know it was that big a deal," Michael stated nervously.

"How did you get paid?" Raul asked, not wanting to hear more of his excuses.

"The money was dropped off in my mailbox by the time I got home from work today."

Raul knew Mercedes' stalker was behind the incident. They were smart to not use any money-transferring technology. Whoever was doing this was local, and Raul had a growing suspicion they had some sort of connection to The Black Kitty.

First, they filmed Mercedes here, and then they chose this location again to have someone scare her. Raul asked Michael more questions, and then sent Johnny to follow the man home and retrieve his online profile information and the remaining bills of the money that Michael hadn't spent yet.

When Michael balked at this plan, Raul reminded him of his promise from earlier, along with a threat of filing charges against him for stalking and harassment. Michael made the wise choice to oblige Raul and Johnny.

Raul then left to return to Mercedes' changing room. As he walked down the hall, he was passed by one of The Black Kitty employees, but he didn't know her name.

"Who was that?" Raul asked Lorenzo.

"Name's Roxxy. She's what they call a stage kitten. She brings all the discarded costumes to the girls," Lorenzo said, lifting up Mercedes' costume in his hands.

"I'll take this to her. I'm going to have her get dressed and then head out. Wait by the back exit for us," Raul instructed, as he knocked on the door.

"Mercedes, it's me," he called through the door.

When she opened the door, Raul felt his heart tug at the look of worry and strain. He didn't like seeing that expression on her beautiful face, but he needed to be honest with her.

Raul told her everything Michael told him, before leaving the room to allow her to get dressed. Fifteen minutes later, Raul placed his hand at the small of Mercedes' back while they walked down the hall and out the back exit.

Lorenzo held the door as they walked into the warm night air. Raul, ever vigilant, scanned the parking lot and the vehicles, making sure there was no one hiding out or around. He opened the door for Mercedes, and once she was in, he closed her door and hurried to the driver's side to head home.

Within thirty minutes they were pulling up to his gated community. He was let in the gate by the guard, and drove a few blocks to his house. Once he pulled up and turned off the ignition, he looked over at Mercedes, who'd remained silent the whole ride.

"Hey." He turned her head to face him. "I'm not going to let anything happen to you. You know that, right?"

A faint smile appeared across Mercedes face and she nodded. "I know. I trust you."

Raul's heart swelled with emotion at hearing those words. After opening the car door, he got out and then rounded the car to open Mercedes' door.

"Why don't you go up and shower," Raul told her as they entered the house.

She seemed to hesitate, but just as he closed the door and punched in the alarm code, Mercedes turned and cupped his face with her hands. She pulled his head down for a kiss. Raul was stunned for all of two seconds before he pulled her in closer by the waist and deepened the kiss.

He lost track of time as they kissed and felt each other up with their hands. Raul broke away from the kiss and peppered kisses along Mercedes jaw and neck. He nipped lightly at the skin on her neck. She moaned, and he increased the pressure of his nips little by little. He could feel her begin to tremble in his arms.

He pulled away completely.

"You should go up and shower," he said firmly.

Mercedes gave him a confused look, but simply nodded and headed up the stairs. Raul rubbed his hand through his hair as he watched her ascend the steps.

It wasn't that he didn't want her. He wanted her more than he wanted his next breath, but he didn't want her acting out of some need to thank him or some misplaced hero worship. Raul needed her to want him for him.

Raul headed up the stairs to his own room and took a short shower. He let the steam of the warm water penetrate his skin and help sweat away the muscle tension he'd been carrying since that idiot rushed the stage.

He quickly washed himself, then turned off the water. Stepping out, he dried off, and placed the towel around his waist. He sat down on his bed, and pulled out his tablet to write a few emails, but heard a light tap on his door.

"Just a sec," he yelled through the door before throwing on a pair of basketball shorts and a T-shirt.

"You okay?" he asked, opening the door.

Mercedes nodded.

"Did you need something?"

"Yes. You."

Raul's dick jumped at her words and the glint in her eyes. He looked down the length of her body and saw she wore a purple silk negligee. He would bet his entire life's savings she wasn't wearing anything underneath when he saw her nipples pushed against the fabric. He stepped back enough to let her in and closed the door, backing her against it.

"Are you sure this is what you want?" He wanted her to be absolutely sure because he couldn't hold out much longer. He watched as a confused shadow cloud Mercedes' face. "I don't want you feeling like you owe me this or you reacting out of the heightened adrenaline because of what happened at the club tonight."

Realization dawned on her, and she smiled. She reached up on her tiptoes and pulled his head down for a quick kiss on the lips.

"If you recall, this is a continuation of what happened earlier tonight at dinner, *before* we left for the club. I don't want to think about a stalker or anything else tonight. I just want you." She whispered the last part as she kissed along his jawline.

Her admission, along with the feel of her lips and hands on him, caused Raul to lose control on the tiny bit of restraint he had. He pressed his lips firmly to hers, biting at her lips, demanding they part for him.

When they did, he showed her no mercy.

He placed an all-out assault on all her senses. He kissed her lips and then moved down to her neck, sucking and biting, as his hands wound their way under her negligee. Just as he assumed, she wore nothing underneath, and when his fingers grazed over her warm mound, he felt Mercedes' heavy intake of breath.

Raul wasted no time … he bent down, wrapping his hands around her thighs and picking her up. Obliging, she twined her legs around his waist. He easily strode to his bed, and placed her on his gray, Frette sheets.

"You better be sure about this because I'm not letting you up for air until sometime tomorrow," he said as he gazed down at her body.

Mercedes smiled mischievously. "Less talking, more showing."

Raul growled as he climbed over her. "My fucking pleasure."

CHAPTER 12

Fire burned through Mercedes' body when Raul's weight pressed her into the bed. He leaned down, leaving soft kisses on her lips, neck, and ear. She tilted her head up to grant him better access to her neck.

He felt so good on top of her.

His fingers pushed the straps of her negligee down her arms and exposed her breasts.

Mercedes barely had time to register the cool air that touched her nipples before she felt them pushed together and surrounded by the warmth of Raul's mouth.

She moaned loudly.

Her breasts were one of the most sensitive spots on her body. As Raul sucked and massaged her breasts, her pussy grew wetter. Mercedes intertwined her fingers in his hair, pulling him closer, as she pushed her breasts even deeper into his mouth.

"Raul," she moaned.

Mercedes gasped when he slowly moved his mouth off her breast, causing a "pop" when he finally released it. He grabbed her wrists and forced them over her head.

"Grab the headboard," he commanded. "Don't move your hands," he said sternly. He eased his way down her body, kissing a trail from her breasts down to where she needed him most. She spread her legs wider when his warm breath grazed along the short curls that covered her sex.

His strong fingers played in her pubic hairs, and then moved down her wet core, spreading her moisture around her pussy.

Instead of diving in, Raul placed kisses on Mercedes' inner thighs and pelvic bone, teasing her with his fingers and the feel of his tongue, close but not close enough to where she wanted.

"Raauuul," she moaned again, this time lifting her hips to encourage him to put his mouth on her.

"Shhh, querida. I know what you need," he said in a voice that made Mercedes' pussy muscles tighten.

Raul teased her some more, before finally putting his lips on her. He kissed and licked around her clit, then took the bud fully into his mouth, stroking it over and over with his tongue.

At the same time, he inserted two fingers into her soaking wet core, and pumped them in tandem with the movement of his tongue. Mercedes thrashed her head on the pillows and began to loosen her grip on the headboard. She moved her hips up and down while Raul continued to feast on her.

Unable to take it any longer, she moved her hands down to her breasts, pinching her nipples.

By now Raul had inserted a third finger into her canal, and continued sucking on her clit. Mercedes forgot all about her breasts and moved both hands to cup the back of Raul's head, holding him in place. She didn't have to worry about him going anywhere, though. He was a man on a mission.

As Raul sucked and finger fucked her, Mercedes felt the muscles in her pussy tighten right before she was overtaken by a heavenly sensation.

"Oh Godddd. Fuck. I'm coming!" she cried out. Ripple after ripple of sensation passed through her and she was powerless to do anything but lay there and surrender to the feeling. Her hands fell away from

Raul's head, and she laid there with her eyes half closed, catching her breath.

She saw Raul rise up with a smirk on his face.

"Querida, I told you to keep your hands on the headboard," he shook his head, reprimanding her.

Mercedes had no time to defend her actions before he yanked her negligee all the way off and flipped her on her belly, pulling her up by the waist so she was on all fours.

"Not listening. That deserves a spanking, and you can watch."

Mercedes was confused about the last part of his statement, until he gently pulled her head back, causing her to look up. The entire door frame of his large walk-in closet was a full-length mirror.

She gasped when she saw the reflection of the wanton expression on her face as she was perched on all fours on Raul's bed, naked as the day she was born, while Raul knelt behind her. Mercedes' breasts grew heavy with need and desire. Raul, who was shirtless, looked in the mirror directly into her gaze.

Mercedes licked her lips just as she saw Raul's hand rise.

"Ahhhh," she yelped, then moaned as his hand made contact with her behind.

Smack!

"Mmmm," Mercedes moaned and pushed back into Raul, continuing to stare at their reflections in the mirror. She'd been intimate plenty of times before, but never had she felt this lascivious as she stared at them both in the mirror, and braced for another smack on her ass.

By the third slap, Mercedes felt the burning sensation on her ass, and she assumed she'd have trouble sitting the next day, but she was too far gone to care.

However, Raul was a giving lover. He never let a woman walk away from his bed unsatisfied. He bent down and kissed the reddened spots on Mercedes' ass cheeks, licking to soothe them. He moved lower to lick and taste her pussy lips, which were now even wetter than before.

He smiled knowingly. She enjoyed being spanked. Mercedes

ground her hips onto Raul's face as he worked his lips and his tongue. Before long, he couldn't stand it any longer.

"Don't move. And this time don't even think of disobeying me." His voice was tight with need and desire. He pulled away from her and stepped off the bed.

Mercedes knew when to comply. She kept her ass perched high in the air, as she watched him in the mirror. He tugged his shorts down and retrieved a handful of condoms out of his top dresser drawer.

She saw him rip open the wrapper and roll the condom down his thick cock. When he moved behind her, keeping his gaze trained on hers in the mirror, she saw the promise in his eyes. Mercedes knew he meant every word he'd said earlier about not letting her up until sometime the next day.

Even as that thought registered in her mind, she felt the bed dip, and Raul's hands were on her hips.

In one swift motion he thrust his cock into her wet core. She gasped and she heard Raul say something in Portuguese, which she couldn't understand, but fuck if it didn't turn her on even more. Within seconds he was pounding into her. Showing her no mercy as he rode her hard.

"Aww shit, querida," he yelled, as Mercedes met him thrust for thrust. "That's it. Take this dick. Take all of it."

Mercedes had no choice but to comply as her hips involuntarily pushed back onto Raul's hardness. Raul continued to pound into Mercedes while he moved his hands around to massage her breasts. He pulled her up, so that her back met his chest, and he moved in and out of her wetness.

Mercedes let her head fall back on Raul's shoulder as she moaned and covered his hands with hers. The quivering of Mercedes' thighs signaled that she was reaching another climax.

"Look in the mirror, baby. I want to see you come," Raul said in her ear.

Mercedes lifted her head and stared at their reflection in the mirror. Raul moved a hand down to stroke her clit.

"This pussy feels so good. So tight and wet. Is that for me?" Raul asked, staring at her reflection.

When Mercedes nodded, he began to move his hand vigorously over her clit, and Mercedes couldn't hold back her second orgasm. She came looking him in the eye in the mirror, calling his name.

The contraction of her muscles around his cock signaled his own orgasm. He pulled her even closer to him and pumped furiously, shouting loudly as he released into the condom.

"Fuuuuck!" he shouted.

They both fell back to the bed, exhausted but completely sated. Raul tugged Mercedes under him, and placed kisses on her lips and face. He pulled back and just stared at her.

"That was …" His voice trailed off.

"I know," she agreed, not needing him to finish his sentence. He smiled and kissed her again before rolling off the bed and heading to the bathroom.

A few minutes later, he came back with a warm cloth and wiped her down, then cleaned himself off. He dropped the cloth in his laundry bin and climbed into bed with Mercedes.

"I hope you know you're getting rounds tonight, so I'd advise you to sleep while you can," he said as he turned them on their sides.

Mercedes giggled.

"Yes, sir." She sighed when she felt his cock twitch upon her calling him sir.

"Don't tease me or you're in trouble," he said, swiftly smacking her on her behind.

"Noted."

* * *

RAUL WOKE up the next day a satisfied man. He looked over at the clock to see it was just after twelve noon. He and Mercedes had gone at it all night long and well into the morning. First, he'd rode Mercedes hard and long, and then she turned the tables and rode him the same way.

He smiled and stretched as he remembered the feel of being inside of her. He inhaled deeply, taking in her scent on his sheets. Looking down, he saw her nestled against his chest, sleeping like a baby. He ran his hand up and down her arm, and placed a kiss on her forehead.

"Hey, sleepyhead. Wake up," he said, just above a whisper.

"Let me sleep." She waved him off.

Raul wouldn't give up, though.

He flipped her onto her back, looking down at her exposed breasts. He could see marks where he'd suckled at her skin. He pressed a kiss between her breasts before moving down her body. He could feel her breathing increase as her senses woke up. When he reached her core, he placed her legs on his shoulders and leaned down, stopping just above her clit.

"You sure you want me to let you sleep?" he teased.

"You better not get me hot and bothered for nothing," she answered breathlessly.

Raul laughed as he lowered his head all the way to her pussy and placed his lips on her. Mercedes moaned instantly. He kissed and nipped at her pussy lips, opting to forego sucking her clit for a little while longer.

He licked the length of her core, before dipping his tongue inside of her wetness. Placing his hands on either side of her waist, he held her in place as she ground her hips against his mouth. Raul licked and stroked her clit with his tongue, then pulled it between his lips.

He inserted two fingers into her, curling them to graze her G-spot. Soon, she was shouting his name as she came. The sound of his name as it was yelled from her lips caused his already growing length to become hard as steel. He quickly grabbed a condom, sheathed himself, and pushed into Mercedes' warm channel before she had time to recover from her orgasm.

He fucked her hard and fast, taking her face between his hands and pressing kisses all over her face. Mercedes grasped his shoulders and pulled him down for a kiss, as she simultaneously planted her feet on the bed and lifted her hips. It was the same move she did on stage, the one Raul had fantasized about her doing as he was balls deep inside of her. Now that he was here, it felt better than he could have imagined. He reached down and rolled her clit between his thumb and forefinger.

Soon they both fell over the edge together, moaning and writhing against one another as they came. And just that fast, they both fell back in bed, Mercedes curling up under Raul's arm. They both fell asleep lying with their limbs entwined with one another.

Two hours later, both were up and showered, sharing a late lunch of Mexican takeout. Mercedes hungrily munched on her rice and bean burrito with a side of roasted vegetables, while Raul ate his chicken tacos. Mercedes opted to cancel her performance at The Black Kitty given the events of the previous night.

She refused to cancel any of her out-of-town performances, but she wanted to play it safe when it came to performing at The Black Kitty. Raul had asked her about the different performers at the club, the employees, and anyone she regularly came in contact with while there.

The list was long, but he felt it was important to check out all possibilities. He was still looking for an ex-girlfriend of hers named Sharon. She was from Savannah, but when Raul's team looked her up, they'd found she had moved and left no forwarding address. Her move happened to be around the same time Mercedes started receiving hang up calls.

Given that Sharon also knew Mercedes regularly performed at The Black Kitty, and had been to her apartment while they dated, he thought they might have the right suspect.

But he held off on drawing any conclusions until he spoke with her, which he couldn't do until they found her.

"I want you to teach me self-defense," Mercedes stated, interrupting his thoughts.

He sat back in his chair. "You sure?"

"Yeah. I mean, I've taken kickboxing for a few years, so I know some stuff, but I want to learn more. You also said you would teach me capoeira. That's self-defense, right?"

Raul nodded. "It's one form, yes. But not always useful in certain situations. I can teach you some capoeira, and other self-defense moves that incorporate more hand strikes, elbows, and takedowns."

Mercedes looked excited. "Can we start today?"

Raul laughed at her enthusiasm. "Yes."

Later that night the pair stood in Raul's upstairs gym panting and sweating, as they sipped from their Avian bottles of water. He'd thoroughly gone over a series of defense moves including palm strikes, kicks, elbow throws, and finger lock takedowns.

And that was before he even began the teaching of capoeira.

Raul had taught her the basic theme of Capoeira was trickery. To catch an opponent off-guard, you must trick them into thinking one thing, while plotting a different course of action.

Once finished with their self-defense training, Raul offered to rub Mercedes down in his Jacuzzi-style bath, and when she happily agreed, Raul strolled over to her with a sexy glint in his eyes

"You know how fine you look half naked, sweaty, and breathing all heavy?" he whispered in her ear.

She wore a pair of blue running shorts and just a black sports bra, for easy moving during their workout.

"If it's half as sexy as you look, then I'd say we're both in trouble," she retorted.

Mercedes was as turned on as he was, as she stared at the rippling muscles in his chest and stomach. He'd worn a pair of gray sweatpants and a white T-shirt, but had discarded the T-shirt some time during their workout.

Mercedes had barely been able to concentrate on his teachings, as she daydreamed of licking the sweat that ran down his neck, over his chest, and through the peaks and valleys of his stomach muscles.

She was so caught up in her fantasy once again, she didn't realize how close Raul was. Before she knew it, he'd taken the nearly empty water bottle from her hand, tossed it in the trash, and thrown her over his shoulder. She didn't have time to catch her breath before she felt his hand make contact with her upturned bottom.

Smack!

"Ouch!" she yelped. "What was that for?" she asked, caught off guard.

"That was for making me look like a bad teacher. I just spent two hours teaching you to defend yourself and look how easily I caught you off guard. That won't do, querida," he reprimanded her as he carried her like a sack of potatoes to his bathroom.

He placed her feet on the floor next to the bath.

"Maybe, you're not as good of a teacher as you like to think," she taunted, placing her hand on her hip.

"Or maybe you're just dickmatized," he said before cupping her face with his hands.

Mercedes refused to respond to his comment because she feared he was right. She'd spent more than a year and a half fantasizing about Raul, three weeks living in his home, countless kisses, but just one night in his bed and she knew this relationship was unlike any other she'd ever had.

Instead of saying all that to him, she gave in to the kiss he placed against her lips as he removed her clothing. It would be a long time before they emerged from the bathtub, wrinkled as prunes, but thoroughly satisfied.

CHAPTER 13

aul woke up early Saturday morning to a ringing phone.

"Bom dia, filho." Before Raul even had a chance to greet his mother, he heard another voice on the line.

"Good morning, Raul."

Raul had to stop himself from groaning.

His mother, along with Iris Collins, Nikola's mother and for all intents and purposes, his second mother, were both on the line. This could only spell trouble. Whenever the two tag teamed him like this it usually had something to do with his love life.

"We know you're in Chicago on business, filho, but we wanted to catch up. You never call your mother anymore. How are you doing? Are you working too hard? Are you eating well?" Raul's mother asked in her concerned voice.

Once again, before Raul could even get a word out, he was interrupted.

"Same here. He never calls or comes by to visit his second mother. Even though we live in the same city." Raul heard the admonishment in Iris' voice.

"Filho, is this true?" his mother asked.

Of course it's not true. I speak with you both at least once a week, he wanted to say, but held his tongue.

"No, Mama. I've just been busy with work. You know that's why I'm in Chicago now."

It had been three weeks since Mercedes and Raul's first explosive night together, and they were now in Chicago for more performances of hers. They'd gotten in the night before, and spent a good part of the night doing some very inappropriate things to each other's bodies before falling into a dreamless sleep.

But he couldn't tell his two mothers that. So, as he eased from under a still sleeping Mercedes, and walked into the living room area of their hotel, closing the bedroom door behind him, he merely listened to the two women as they talked.

"Yes, Nikola says you are working with a friend of Devyn's. Is that right?"

That damn Nikola.

He and Devyn were still in Brazil for the summer, and likely spent time visiting his parents, who were like second parents to Nikola. His friend knew telling his mother he was working with Mercedes would pique her interest.

"Oh, you mean Mercedes?" Iris interjected. "Are you helping her, Raul?"

In more ways than one. Again, he opted not to share those thoughts with the two women.

"Yes, Mama Iris. I'm helping Mercedes. She's had a little trouble," he said, not wanting to go into full details.

"And how is that going?" his mother asked, but he could hear an underlying curiosity in her voice. She wanted to know if it was more than just business.

"It's going fine. We're in Chicago for, uh, her work, and I'm here to make sure she remains safe."

"Oh, son, you don't have to hold back, we both know Mercedes performs burlesque. That cat was out of the bag a long time ago. She's absolutely fabulous, too. She's beautiful and the godmother of my grandbabies, Rosaline. You have to meet her," Iris announced excitedly.

Raul wasn't surprised Iris knew Mercedes was a burlesque dancer, she'd surprised Nikola and Devyn with the news she'd been to a number of Devyn's shows. Being from Brazil, and growing up attending Carnival, he knew his mother wasn't uncomfortable with women dressing in a way some in the US would call scandalous, for the public.

He'd grown up seeing his mother, and other family relatives decked out in their Carnival costumes, elaborately decorated, and women dancing freely in the streets.

"Oh, Iris, tell me about her," Raul's mother demanded.

"Well, like I said she's godmother to Theodore and Jacques. She and Devyn went to college together, and she is beautiful …"

Raul drowned out the two women as he stared out the hotel's window, down onto the Chicago streets.

It was only eight in the morning, so there were few people out and about.

Raul thought about his nervousness for Mercedes' performance that night. Since his employees were busy with other assignments, he didn't have any backup with him in Chicago. The summer was in full swing and many of his high-end clients wanted extra security for their parties and getaways.

Raul usually traveled a great deal during this time of the year with his top clients, but he'd made Mercedes his priority, for reasons he didn't want to analyze at the moment. Especially, not with both his mothers on the phone speculating as to what was going on.

Raul turned as he heard the creak of the bedroom door open. He licked his lips when he saw Mercedes standing there dressed in the dress shirt he'd stripped out of the night before in his rush to feel her skin against his. The bottom of the shirt skimmed the tops of her thighs.

Her sight of her thighs caused his mouth to water. His fingers itched to press against them. Forgetting the conversation happening on his phone, he took a step toward Mercedes.

"So, you're just working with this Mercedes, filho?" Rosaline's question halted his movement. At the same time, Mercedes realized he was on the phone, and whispered she would be in the bedroom.

"Is that her?"

Damn.

His mother had hearing like a damn cat. Nothing ever got past the woman.

"It's quite early in the morning, no?" she asked, half reprimanding, half joyfully.

He knew how badly his mother wanted him to marry and have a family she could love. Usually thinking of the m-word made his heart race anxiously, but this time he didn't have that reaction.

Again, he chose to wonder about the reason why later.

Much later.

"Yes, it's early here, Mama, but security is a twenty-four-hour job," he said cryptically.

"Mmhm, I bet it is," both Iris and his mother said at the same time.

The two women had formed a unique bond in the decades since Nikola and Raul had become friends. When Iris' husband was killed in a car accident years before, Raul's mother had stayed with Iris for weeks, as she grieved.

They also bonded over lamenting that their sons were unmarried. Now that Nikola was married with a family, the two women focused on Raul, and Nikola's younger brother, Andre. Neither woman would be satisfied until their boys were in love and married.

Raul shook his head.

The trio talked for another ten minutes, mostly focused on the two women inquiring about his relationship with Mercedes, and Raul working hard to evade their answers. Raul had to use nearly every evasion technique he learned in the military and work as a security specialist to escape this conversation without his mother and Iris going out and searching for a wedding planner.

He thought, *If the US is really serious about the War on Terrorism, they should send Iris Collins and Rosaline Santiago into question suspects. If they* both knew the depth of his feelings for Mercedes, they'd surely up their campaign to see him married in the near future.

After reassuring both women he would make sure to call them more often, they, thankfully, let him off the phone.

He walked into the bedroom to find Mercedes lying in the center of the bed, propped up on her elbows, knees bent, and legs apart. From where he stood, he could see that she wasn't wearing any panties. He licked his lips as he stared into what he'd come to call the center of Heaven.

"So, security is a twenty-four-hour job, huh?" she asked, spreading her legs even wider.

Raul nodded. "It was either that or tell my two mothers I had you up half the night screaming my name."

"Oh really? 'Cause if memory serves, I heard my name called a few times."

"You sure? I don't remember that," Raul said, leaning his head to the side as if trying to recall a memory.

Mercedes slid off the king-sized bed and came to stand in front of him.

"Let me remind you."

She rose up on her tiptoes, and placed a kiss on his lips, then moved down to his neck. She slowly ran her tongue along his collarbone, and Raul's cock was instantly hard. She heard a low groan above her. She'd learned that licking and sucking on his collarbone was one of his sweet spots.

Mercedes ran her hand up and down his bare chest, while she moved down to twirl her tongue around one nipple then the other. Painstakingly slow, she kissed down his torso until she was on her knees in front of him. Tucking her thumbs into the waistband of his sweatpants, she pushed them down his lean hips.

Raul wore no underwear, and his cock sprang out of his pants.

For a second, she thought of teasing him, until she looked up into his eyes. The need she saw in his gaze penetrated to her core. Mercedes used her tongue to spread the pearl of pre-cum that emerged from the tip of his shaft.

Deciding against taking it slow, Mercedes fit her lips around his girth and sucked him into her mouth. Raul groaned even louder as his head fell back against the wall behind him. At first, Mercedes let her moistened lips caress up and down his shaft, but when she felt Raul's hands in her hair, encouraging her for more, she upped the ante.

Mercedes allowed her tongue to glide along the underside of his cock, while she hollowed her cheeks and sucked.

She could already feel the weight of his cock grow heavier in her mouth as it filled with come. She placed her hands on each of his butt and deepened her sucking. She knew Raul was on the edge when his grip tightened in her hair, but she pulled back, releasing his cock. Before Raul could protest, she dipped her head lower, sucking his balls into her mouth, and using one hand to continue stroking his length.

Mercedes continued this for a few moments, before returning her mouth's attention back to his cock. She quickened her pace, and took him to the back of her throat. She used one hand to massage his balls, as she let her tongue toy with his cock.

Within minutes, she felt his balls draw up, before his cock bulged even more.

"Shit. Fuck. Mercedes!" Raul yelled above her, just as his semen splashed against her tongue.

She continued to suckle him until the very last drop. When he stopped coming, Mercedes felt him slump against the wall, as she stood up.

"You remember now?" she asked in response to his teasing from earlier.

Raul watched as she turned and walked toward the bathroom, unbuttoning and removing his shirt as she went. Just as she made it to the door, she peered over her shoulder.

"You coming?"

He knew this woman was going to be the death of him, but he'd go out a happy man.

Raul half-smiled as he summoned the will to push himself from the wall, remove his sweatpants, and follow her into the bathroom.

* * *

CHRISSY, one of the stage kittens at the Chicago club, yelled out, "Knock 'em dead, Dahlia!"

Mercedes had performed there every summer, and a few holiday weekends throughout the year, for the past few years. The regular performers and owners had come to know her face, and greatly respected her as a performer. She'd just stepped out of her private changing room, to find Chrissy ogling Raul, as he waited for her.

The sense of possessiveness she felt had grown exponentially in the past few weeks.

Mercedes usually wasn't a jealous or possessive partner. In the past, if a partner of hers had a wandering eye, she'd let them go without much fanfare. But with Raul, she'd see random women eyeing him and she found herself pulling him closer or putting his arm around her waist just to let those women know he was taken.

It baffled her how much she'd come to care for him in a short period of time. Truthfully, it scared the hell out of her. She'd come to know the Raul underneath the exterior. Yes, he was gorgeous, successful, and extremely charming, but he was also compassionate, family-oriented, and one of the smartest people she'd ever met.

He'd opened up his home to keep her safe, and shared stories of his family and growing up in Brazil, his time in college, and in the Army.

For her part, Mercedes told him bits and pieces of her childhood, stories of her time at college in Washington DC, and what drove her to try burlesque once she had her own independence.

She didn't go into detail about her relationship with her parents or how strict her father was on her, while he had countless extramarital affairs.

If she shared that, she'd also have to share her fear of commitment. Instead, she held that part of her heart from him, fearing if she let him all the way in then she'd have no defenses against falling completely in love with him.

Still, she was afraid that she might be heading in that direction already.

"Thanks, Chrissy," Mercedes said, as she adjusted the pink frills adorning her black corset.

She bent at the waist and smoothed up her black leggings, not because they were wrinkled, but because she knew it would get Raul's attention. When she stood back up, the heated look in his eyes told her she'd accomplished her mission.

"If you want to make it to the stage, you'll cut that out," he whispered in her ear.

Chrissy, seeing the obvious chemistry between the two, opted to head back down the hall in the opposite direction.

Wise choice, Mercedes thought, as she felt Raul's hand at the small of her back, escorting her to the stage area. They'd gone over and over the safety plan for this weekend. Luckily, this stage was set apart from the audience, and a little higher up, making it difficult if anyone decided to jump up on the stage.

Even though Mercedes knew her stalker was still out there, she felt safe as long as Raul was around.

He wouldn't let anything happen to her. Mercedes trusted that with her entire being. Although she hadn't performed at The Black Kitty since that night, she'd performed at other Atlanta area clubs, and in Savannah. Raul was with her every step of the way. As a safety precaution, Mercedes scaled back on the promotional events she often did, and did not tell anyone her schedule.

Though she'd rather be able to join in on the promotional events, she understood the safety concerns and abided by Raul and his team.

When the announcer finally called Black Dahlia to the stage, Mercedes was ready to go.

"Go get 'em, querida," she heard Raul say behind her as his hand slapped her ass.

That man loved to feel on her behind, and she didn't mind one bit. She sent a wink and blew a kiss to him over her shoulder before walking on the stage.

With the spotlight on Mercedes in the darkened club, she forgot about the threats of a stalker, her suspension from her job, and even her fear of commitment. She let all her inhibitions go when she was on stage.

As the sounds of Beyonce's "Lay Up Under Me" began, Mercedes briefly looked to the side of the stage and Raul's face was the first thing she saw. Her moods often dictated her performances.

She chose songs and routines according to how she felt.

She'd spent the past week choreographing a routine to this song because, in spite of herself, the upbeat melody and words of the song fell in line with her growing feelings for Raul. Mercedes crisscrossed the stage, pausing at the edge to give the audience a shimmy of her breasts.

Satisfied with their reaction, she then glided to the other side of the stage, moving her hips and snapping in time with the music.

Mercedes seductively began to unbutton the back of her corset, stopping to tease the audience, before dipping at the waist, doing a flick of her hair, and coming back up in nothing but her black pasties up top. She danced, and spun around, gyrating to the music and feeling free.

The lyrics of the song matched how she felt when she was with Raul. When they were together nothing else mattered. They could lay up under one another, make love well into the night, or laugh together. Mercedes turned and presented the audience with her backside as she popped her hips from side to side in time with the music, letting the frills on her panties move and sway.

Mercedes spun around, dropped to the ground, and hit her signature move, dragging her toes as she moved her hips up toward the ceiling, while supporting her weight on her forearms. She twirled her hips and moved them up and down as the audience clapped and whistled their appreciation.

She loved that burlesque audiences were so responsive. Audience members often competed to see who could applaud the loudest for the performer on stage.

The music last few beats of the song played, and Mercedes dropped down then sat up on her knees, giving the audience one last shake of her pasty-covered breasts, and blew them a kiss.

As euphoric as she felt on stage, that feeling was nothing compared to what she felt as she exited the stage and saw Raul clapping and whistling for her. She instinctively went into his outstretched arms.

When he wrapped his arms around her it felt like coming home.

* * *

"Sir, there's a problem with your room."

Raul quickly opened the door and stepped into the hallway when he saw the worried expression on the hotel's head of security's face.

He knew the man wasn't referring to the room he'd just stepped out of, closing the door behind him. He and Mercedes had returned from her performance, and she'd gone to take a shower when he heard a knock on the door. Peering through the peephole, he saw the tall, bulky frame of the hotel's head of security.

"There was an attempted break-in?" Raul raised his eyebrow at the man.

To throw off anyone who may be following them on their trip, Raul called ahead and had a room reserved under Mercedes' name, and one under an alias he used while working for clients.

Since the first night they spent together, Raul and Mercedes shared rooms, which worked for him for other reasons, but it also was beneficial for Mercedes' safety. Apparently, now someone had tried to track down the dummy reservation that he made under Mercedes' name.

"What happened?" he asked in his no nonsense tone, his instincts on high alert.

"Well, they never actually made it to the room, but one of our staff found that someone tried to break into our computerized guest list using a virus. It was easy to thwart, but we were able to read the encryption of the name they were looking for. It was for a Mercedes Holmes, the same name you reserved a room under," the hotel security specialist told him.

Raul took in this information, his mind spinning with different possibilities.

"Our team is trying to track down the source of the virus, but we're running into some trouble. Though the virus wasn't sophisticated enough to infiltrate our system, sourcing it has still been a problem," the older man stated, a frown marring his face.

"Damn it," Raul cursed under his breath.

He didn't want to leave Mercedes alone to head to the hotel's security office. He knew he and his team could easily source the originator of the virus, but he would need access to the security's system. He and Mercedes were scheduled to leave first thing in the morning.

He didn't want to leave her or alert her if there wasn't any cause to.

Raul quickly thought of a plan to get the information he needed while simultaneously keeping Mercedes in the dark.

"Is there a way for your team to send me the information you have?" Raul asked. "That way, I could analyze the information from my Atlanta office and if necessary send another one of my team members back to Chicago to meet with the security team."

"Yes, sir. We can send you what we've found so far while still continuing our investigation."

"Okay, good. I can begin looking at it tonight, and pass it along to my team. Is everything ready for our checkout in the morning?" Raul asked.

"Yes, sir. Your pre-checkout is taken care of. And your car will be here at seven-thirty sharp to take you and Ms. Holmes to the airport."

"Thank you for all your help," Raul told the man before discussing a few more details of the attempted security breach and then heading into the room.

As he entered the room, Mercedes was just coming out of the bathroom, a plush, white towel wrapped around her wet body, and her hair pulled up into a messy bun on top of her head. She smiled at him as she went to retrieve her mango-scented body butter from the nightstand.

He loved watching as she propped her leg up on the bed and began smearing the off-white cream up and down her smooth legs.

He let his tongue graze his lower lip.

"Who was that at the door?" she asked offhandedly, as she

continued to rub the butter into her leg until it disappeared. She switched legs, propping the other one up and repeating the same motion.

He barely even heard the question as he watched her hand move up her creamy thighs closer to her hip.

"Hello? Raul?" she called

"Hmm?"

"I asked you who was at the door?"

"Security," he responded absentmindedly. He caught himself when he saw her body stiffen and she focused her attention on him.

"Did something happen?"

The worried expression on her face made him mentally kick himself for his gaffe. He hated seeing that look on her face and was determined to erase it. He'd deal with the consequences later.

"No, they came to tell us everything was complete with our early checkout. We're scheduled to leave early tomorrow morning. Now we don't have to worry about stopping by the front desk."

He hoped that explanation appeased her.

"I didn't realize security did that sort of thing. Wouldn't someone from the front desk handle that?" she asked, obviously wondering if this had something to do with whoever was stalking her.

Raul decided to give her a half-truth. "Usually, yes, but since I spoke with security and have a working relationship with this hotel, the front desk runs all their inquiries through the head of security. It's just a precaution."

It wasn't a complete lie, but even so, his gut tightened at the fact that he was keeping her in the dark about this. There were other things she didn't know he was keeping from her as well. *It's for her safety*, he reasoned with himself as he walked over to her and pressed his lips to her forehead.

He moved down to place his face in the crook of her neck and inhaled.

She smelled like the butter cream she'd rubbed into her skin. It reminded him of honey with a hint of spice, a smell that was all Mercedes. He'd come to memorize that scent as it was embedded in all his bed sheets. As far as he was concerned, he could wake up to that smell every day.

"Care for another shower?" he asked, his hand gliding in between the edges of the towel, rubbing circles in her thigh.

"Mmm," she moaned, letting her head fall back, "I just got out of the shower," she said, above a whisper.

Raul let his lips graze hers before speaking. "But you're going to need another one soon. I plan on doing some very dirty things to you over the next few hours," he growled deeply in her ear.

"Hou— Ooh," Mercedes moaned as he inserted a finger into her already damp pussy.

For the rest of the night, he made sure Mercedes forgot all about security and checkout times.

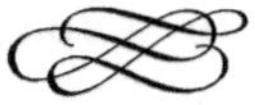

CHAPTER 14

As they ate breakfast in the backyard, Raul asked Mercedes, "Are you ready for today?"

It had been two days since they returned from Chicago, and the morning they arrived home Mercedes got an email from Ron Sherman. The school board was holding a committee meeting on whether to reinstate Mercedes to her job as assistant principal. There were about four weeks until the beginning of the next school year, and Mercedes had a number of performances, the final major one being at the New Orleans Burlesque Festival.

She'd gone for the past few years. They would be staying in New Orleans for a week, taking in shows, and Mercedes had three performances scheduled for that week. Nikola and Devyn were even going to meet the pair in the city to hang out for a few days.

But first, Mercedes and Raul were attending her committee hearing to find out if she would have a job to return to. Raul could sense her nervousness.

"I'm as ready as I can be." She let out a humorless laugh. "You know what's funny? Before all of this, I started to question if my career in education was for me. Like if working in education was my destiny forever, but having the threat of it being taken away, I realize how much it means to me.

"I still love performing, and if I wanted, I could probably perform full-time, but I enjoy the balance education and performing provide in my life. I'm not just Mercedes Holmes the assistant principal or Black Dahlia burlesque dancer. I'm both."

Raul pushed a loose curl behind her ear and let his finger graze along the lower line of her jaw.

"Then be both," he said, gazing into the brown pools of her eyes.

He felt his stomach turn with a feeling he'd never felt before looking into her eyes. When she smiled at him and placed a light kiss on the hand that had been stroking her face, his heart nearly tumbled out of his chest and right onto her lap. He was hers for the taking and he hoped she knew it.

"I will." She smiled at him. "I just want this to be over."

For a second, he thought she was referring to the committee hearing, until he realized she was referring to this whole ordeal.

Mercedes was tired of living under the threat of someone stalking her. He still hadn't told her about what happened in Chicago. He had his team working on the source of the attempted security breach. After some work by his team, they found out that the source of the break-in originated in Chicago.

Raul had casually asked Mercedes if she knew anyone in the city, outside of the burlesque world, and she told him she didn't. The more they found out, the more Raul speculated whoever this was, was someone in her burlesque circle.

Someone she'd beaten in a competition, perhaps? Or someone who believed she didn't belong? He wasn't sure, but he was working to find out.

"It will be over. We'll get whoever is doing this," he reassured her.

"You don't still think it could be Sharon, do you?" she asked about her ex-girlfriend.

Raul thought she may have something to do with this when his team couldn't locate her in the Savannah apartment she'd lived in while dating Mercedes. It took his team a little while to track the woman down, but they had.

Raul shook his head. "We found her. She's living in Southern California." Raul actually had a video call with Sharon the day before.

"California? What's she doing there?" Mercedes asked, perplexed.

"Her mother moved out there a few years ago, and she's fallen ill. Sharon moved in to take care of her," Raul stated.

Mercedes' hand covered her mouth. It'd been a while since she spoke to Sharon, but she was saddened to hear of her mother being ill. She wondered why she hadn't seen Sharon at the usual burlesque shows this year.

"Is she going to be okay? Her mother, I mean?" Mercedes asked.

Raul lifted his shoulder in a shrug. "I'm not sure, querida. She's pretty sick."

Raul had his team verify Sharon's claims through electronic medical records. Legally, he couldn't tell her his team hacked Sharon's mother's medical records, but it'd confirmed Sharon's story.

"Do you have her address?"

Raul pulled back, looking at Mercedes. He wondered if she was thinking of trying to visit her.

"Her address?"

Mercedes nodded. "Yes. I would like to send her flowers or something. She's an only child, so I know it's got to be hard seeing her mother so ill. She and I aren't exactly friends, but she is someone I cared for when we were dating."

Raul nodded. He understood. Mercedes may have her hang-ups about commitment, and he'd definitely picked up on that, but she was a good woman with a kind heart.

"Yes, I have her address. We can even stop by the flower shop after the hearing, if you'd like," he promised.

His heart leapt again at the smile she gave him. What he wouldn't give to wake up to that smile every morning.

Wait ... what?

He'd been having that thought more and more lately.

"Let's go." He rose abruptly, helping Mercedes to her feet from her seat.

They loaded their breakfast dishes in the dishwasher and made their way out the door to the meeting.

* * *

MERCEDES FOLLOWED behind Raul as they entered the main office of her school, where the board members decided to have this meeting.

"You can wait out in the lobby," one of the board members, Mr. Roberts, told Raul as he stood at the door.

Mercedes turned to peer at Raul over her shoulder. In a flash his facial expression went from relaxed to menacing.

Raul stepped forward. "I'm not leaving her side, and if you try to make me, you're going to have a serious problem on your hands." He smiled at Roberts but there was nothing friendly about it.

Mercedes cleared her throat. "It's a safety measure," she assured the board member, along with the others, not wanting to go into full details. She pushed out a sigh of relief when Roberts backed down and stepped aside, letting Raul pass by.

Mercedes took her seat at the end of the long table.

Around the table sat Ron, Superintendent Walters, Roberts, and two other members of the board of directors, who Mercedes had been introduced to at previous events. Mercedes couldn't read the expressions on the older men's faces.

Raul sat off to the side of the room, as an observer.

Mercedes felt a deep sense of gratitude for Raul's protection, even though she believed she wasn't in danger from the people in this room. Just his presence, knowing she had someone in her corner, literally and figuratively, helped her confidence. She unconsciously looked over at Raul for reassurance, and he winked at her and nodded ever so slightly.

His non-verbal way of telling her everything would be okay. He did the same move whenever she was on stage and she glanced at him. Though she never got nervous on stage anymore, his little reassurances gave her a more ebullient step while performing. It did the same thing now and she knew she had to say something.

Mercedes cleared her throat. "I'd like the opportunity to speak before you make your ruling," she stated, head held up proudly.

The board of director's members looked at one another, and then one nodded to Superintendent Walters. Finally, she spoke, "Yes, Ms. Holmes, you may have your say."

Mercedes pushed back her chair and stood, with her head held high.

"First, I'd like to say it has been a privilege to work at this school for the last seven years. The first five I spent in the classroom shaping young minds, and the last two on the administration side being able to mold our curriculum and mentor young teachers. It is a career I always took seriously and would never do anything to disrespect.

"As you all have recently discovered, in addition to my career in education, I also work as a burlesque dancer and have for a number of years. Dancing and performing is a passion of mine, and I love it as much as I love working with our students. I have never and would never do anything to jeopardize my career as an educator.

"I recently questioned whether or not I wanted to continue on this career path. I believed that I maybe saw it as a safe career track. I toyed with the idea of working burlesque full-time, but I have come to the conclusion that I love my job. Teaching, education, and watching young children accomplish dreams they never knew they had, fills my heart with joy, and it would hurt me to the core of my being to not be able to do that."

Mercedes paused, looking pointedly at each individual at the table. She couldn't see him, but somehow she knew Raul was watching her with pride and inwardly smiling.

"I want to keep my job, but I won't do it at the expense of my performing either," she continued, noticing the surprised looks of the people at the table. Apparently, they were stunned to find out she had no intention of throwing herself at their mercy.

No matter how much she wanted her career, she wouldn't compromise herself.

"I am an educator, but I'm also a performer. I love performing as much as I love teaching. I am talented and skilled at both, and I plan to continue to do both, whether that is here or at a different school. I'm sorry if some of the parents have a hard time with that, but I am an adult who has a life outside of these walls. I have found a balance in my life, and I enjoy it. I won't apologize for any of it."

She paused, once again looking around the table.

"Thank you," she concluded her speech and sat back down.

For a full minute there was silence in the room as the committee looked at one another around the table. Mercedes was no longer concerned with reading their faces.

She'd meant every word she said. She knew she was a talented educator and could find another position at a different school. It would be tough leaving her colleagues and the students she'd mentored since starting at the school, but she would do it if she had to.

"Thank you for those words, Mercedes," Ron was the first to speak.

"We will need a few minutes to discuss among ourselves. If you don't mind, can you and, uh, your guest please have a seat in the outer office?" Superintendent Walters interjected, looking between Mercedes and Raul.

The two stood, and without hesitation, Raul wrapped his arm around her waist, opening the door for her. With her back to the room, Mercedes missed the hard glare Raul sent over his shoulder at those remaining seated in the conference room, but they didn't miss it.

"You can be my teacher anytime, querida," he said, pulling her into his warm embrace once the door closed behind them.

She wrapped her arms around his strong back and let her head rest on his shoulder, not caring if anyone saw them.

"Thank you," she nearly whispered.

"For what? I didn't do anything."

"Yes, you did." She squeezed her arms around his body even tighter. Closing her eyes, she inhaled deeply. No matter the committee's ruling she would be all right.

* * *

A FEW HOURS LATER, Raul and Mercedes were in good spirits as they waited for Iris Collins to answer her door. Mercedes had been reinstated to her position as assistant principal. After the committee meeting, Raul took Mercedes to a local flower shop to send a bouquet to Sharon out in California.

Now, they were at Iris Collins' condo to have lunch. Iris had moved into Nikola's condominium after he and Devyn moved into their new home.

"Finally, you're here." Iris' smile was a mile wide as she pulled the door open. Her blue eyes sparkled as she looked between Raul and Mercedes. "Come in, come in." She ushered them inside with a wave of her hand.

Mercedes glanced around the modern style furnishings of the home. Iris had chosen an array of off-white and cream-colored furniture and accents to decorate the condo. The natural lighting from the floor-to-ceiling windows combined with the colors gave the condo a very open and warm feeling.

The feeling of the condo mimicked Iris' welcoming demeanor. Though Mercedes had met Iris on numerous occasions, she'd never been to Iris' home. Iris was her usual lively self, showing Mercedes around, asking her about her alter-ego, Black Dahlia. At first, Mercedes was a little uncomfortable talking to the older woman about her dancing, until Iris pulled out an old photo album with pictures of her decked out fishnet stockings, pasties, feather headwear, and very little else.

Seeing the pictures and hearing Iris talk about her years on the burlesque circuit intrigued Mercedes.

They eventually got lost in talking about burlesque, forgetting all about lunch. That is, until Raul cleared his throat.

"Sounds like someone needs attention." Iris raised an eyebrow in Raul's direction.

"You demanded that we come over, claiming you would feed us, and it's been almost an hour," Raul replied.

Iris and Mercedes laughed.

"Trust me, it's best not to keep this guy waiting when it comes to food," Mercedes chimed in.

Iris smirked. "You're right, Raul. I've forgotten my manners, talking to Mercedes about dancing. Have a seat at the dining table, and I'll get us started with the salad." She showed the couple to the dining area that sat in front of a large bay window with a stunning view of downtown Atlanta.

When Mercedes peered up, she spotted Iris watching them with a smirk on her face.

During their lunch of lobster bisque, arugula salad, and rosemary and garlic focaccia bread, the trio continued to talk. Mercedes knew she could never have this type of conversation with her own mother, and certainly not her father.

Her parents would tell her how no man would want her for being a whore and taking her clothes off for money. Her father would remind her of the usual bible verses he quoted her throughout her childhood, to shame her for some perceived indiscretion. He'd admonish her for a while, put her on punishment, and then a few hours later he'd be out the door to meet one of the many women he was having an affair with.

And her mother would, once again, be left behind to go to bed alone at night waiting for her husband to return. Mercedes wasn't aware of the way the sides of her mouth turned down into a frown as she thought of her parents and her father's hypocrisy. But she did notice when she felt Raul staring at her.

His hand slid around hers and squeezed.

"Are you okay?" he asked in a voice laced with concern.

Iris remained quiet, taking in the couple in front of her.

Mercedes forced thoughts of her own family from her head and smiled. "Yes, I'm sorry. I got a little distracted, but I'm all right. I'm sorry, Iris, I didn't mean to check out on you."

"Think nothing of it, sweetie. I know Raul has been helping you with some safety issues you've been having. I'm so sorry you are going through that, but trust and believe our Raul will get to the bottom of it. He's the best at what he does," Iris said proudly.

Mercedes saw the love shining in Iris' eyes as she spoke about Raul. Mercedes could tell Iris loved Raul like she had given birth to him.

"I know he is." Mercedes had let the words slip before she could catch herself.

Iris' laser sharp focus was on Mercedes' hand as it still rested in Raul's larger hand. She was pleased when he brought her hand to his lips for a kiss. She was even more pleased to see Mercedes' features soften into a look of admiration, desire and … love?

She glanced at Raul's face and saw the near identical expression on his face.

It took Iris a mere thirty seconds after Mercedes and Raul left her condo to dial the number for Rosaline in Brazil.

They had a lot to discuss, like whether the wedding should take place in Brazil or Atlanta, because Iris was sure that's where this was headed.

CHAPTER 15

"Raul, this is beautiful. I think it might be too much," Mercedes said as she looked down into the Mississippi River from their hotel suite.

For Mercedes' final burlesque trip of the summer, Raul wanted to do something special for her. Instead of keeping the reservation at the original hotel Mercedes usually stayed at, he'd made a reservation at the upscale Hotel Monteleone.

The room was exquisite, offering a large living room area as soon as you walked in. The room was furnished with a plush, light-colored couch, a couple of floral accented chairs, a flat screen television, and a large window that provided a stunning view of the Mighty Mississippi. But as spacious and accommodating as the living room area was, the bedroom was even more opulent.

A king-sized bed sat at the center of the room, with more windows allowing for a greater view of the river and the city of New Orleans. Booking this suite allowed Raul to kill two birds with one stone.

First, after what happened in Chicago, he didn't want to risk her stalker getting too close to her again. Second, he wanted to do something special for her at the end of their summer of traveling. Raul had become so concerned about keeping Mercedes safe, he'd even thought of asking her to consider skipping this trip altogether, but knew he couldn't do it.

Mercedes talked about getting to New Orleans all summer. It was one of the biggest events in the burlesque world. All the top burlesque performers were expected to be there, including Ditta Von Teese.

After months of living in the shadow of a stalker, Raul couldn't deprive Mercedes of this special trip, so he improvised. He didn't bother to tell her that the room was of no cost to him because his father's company had a standing reservation with the hotel.

Nor did he tell her about the security team he had assigned to them for their time in New Orleans. He went so far as to hire a few outside contractors he worked with to ensure that someone would always be watching their back as they were out and about in the city.

"It's not nearly enough for you, querida," he said, coming up behind her, pulling her back against his chest, and placing a kiss in the crook of her neck.

He instantly felt her relax into her embrace.

"What does that even mean?" she asked.

"What?"

"Querida. You always call me that. I figured it was Portuguese because I've never heard it before. What does it mean?"

Raul smiled.

He'd been calling her 'querida' for months. It just felt as natural as calling her by her name.

"It's just a term of endearment, like 'sweetie' or 'baby' in English," he explained.

Mercedes nodded and turned, looking up at him. "Oh, is that right? So, am I your 'sweetie' or 'baby'?"

Raul stared down into her upturned face.

"Neither, you are my querida." Raul felt her arms tighten around his waist as she laid her head against his chest. From that angle he could see the smile that passed over her face.

Later that evening the couple opted to dine at the hotel's Criollo Restaurant. As they entered the restaurant, Mercedes spotted Jazmine, a regular performer from The Black Kitty.

She dined with an older woman.

"Hey, there's Jazmine," Mercedes told Raul at the same time Jazmine noticed her. She smiled and waved at Mercedes, causing the older woman she was with to turn around.

"Let's go say hi while we wait," she said, grabbing Raul's arm. They had booked a private dining space that the restaurant staff was still readying for them.

"Hey, Jazmine," Mercedes said as they reached her table.

Jazmine stood and greeted Mercedes with a hug and shook hands with Raul upon introduction. She'd met him before at the club, but it was a brief encounter.

The older woman raised an eyebrow. "Jazmine?" she asked.

Mercedes forgot that most of the dancers at The Black Kitty didn't go by their actual names at the club, mostly using their stage names with one another.

"Aunt Ruth, this is the performer I was telling you about, Black Dahlia. We all usually go by our stage names at the club," Jazmine explained to her aunt.

Jazmine's full stage name was Jazmine Noir, but her actual name was Stacey Coleman.

"It's nice to meet you, ma'am. You can call me Mercedes. That's my government name," Mercedes joked, and the table laughed. "This is Raul," she introduced, and Raul shook hands with both the women.

"We didn't want to interrupt, we're waiting for our table and I just saw Jazmine and wanted to say hello."

"Oh, it's no interruption. Sit and have a drink with us while you wait," Jazmine encouraged. "And since we're not at the club, you can call me Stacey."

Raul pulled out a chair for Mercedes and sat in a seat across from her. The waiter came and took their drink orders. Mercedes ordered a white wine, and Raul got a scotch on the rocks.

"I didn't know you were performing here Ja— uh, Stacey," Mercedes said as she sipped from her glass.

Stacey shook her head. "I'm not, but I've wanted to come for a few years now just to watch. This year, my aunt was finally able to take the trip with me." Stacey nodded toward her Aunt Ruth.

"Yup, we're here for the shows, the crawfish, and the beignets," Aunt Ruth said excitedly, causing everyone to laugh.

After another ten minutes of light banter and conversation, the hosts came to let Raul and Mercedes know their dining space was ready.

"Thank you for letting us crash your dinner. Hopefully, we'll get a chance to meet up with one another again before either of us leaves," Mercedes said as she rose from the table.

"That sounds nice. Here, let me give you my cell." Stacey jotted down her cell number on a napkin and handed it to Mercedes.

"Enjoy your dinner and the rest of your night." Stacey's aunt smiled as the pair left following the host.

* * *

"You didn't know she was going to be here?" Raul asked as they sat down to their table in the private dining room.

Mercedes shook her head. "No, but it was nice to see her."

Raul nodded. "And you didn't tell anyone where you were staying, right?"

Mercedes looked up at Raul in confusion. "How could I tell anyone? I didn't even know we were staying here until we arrived, remember?" she asked, getting curious.

Raul had kept their hotel reservation a secret from everyone including her. Mercedes was starting to feel like he was holding something back from her.

"Is something the matter? And don't lie to me," she told him.

"And you haven't told anyone since we've been here, right?" he asked, ignoring her last statement.

"No, Raul. I haven't told anyone. I haven't even talked to anyone else," she said, tension growing in her voice.

"Okay." He blew out a breath.

Mercedes felt whatever he was preparing to say she wasn't going to like.

"When we were in Chicago, there was an attempted security breach," he stated calmly.

"What kind of security breach?"

"Someone tried to hack into the hotel's guest list and get the room number you were staying in. They weren't successful, and security immediately came and told me. Even if they found your name on the guest list, they would have had the wrong room.

"I placed your name on the list as a decoy, and booked the room we actually stayed in under an alias. You were never in any danger." Raul took a moment to let what he'd just said sink in, before telling her more.

He figured if he was going to be upfront, he might as well tell the whole truth.

"There's more," he said.

Mercedes peered at him intently, waiting for him to finish.

"There've been letters. Your stalker has been sending letters to your PO box for the past few months. My team has been intercepting them," he explained.

"What do the letters say?"

Raul didn't want to say the vile filth that was contained in the letters. They were filled with threats of violence and innuendos blaming her for the destruction of a family. Raul had spoken with all her recent exes, and even some from her past. None of them had been married or even had children. Mercedes was definitely nobody's homewrecker, so he couldn't understand how this person blamed her for the breakup of a family.

"You don't need to know about that," he tried to mollify her.

"Don't need to know?" she asked incredulously.

"Mercedes, calm down."

As soon as the words left his mouth, he knew he'd made a mistake. Any man with a decent grasp of human behavior knew that telling a woman to *calm down* when she was upset only had the opposite effect.

"Don't tell me to calm the fuck down. I'm the one who's being sent threatening letters! What if this sicko had gotten my room number in

Chicago? Why didn't you tell me? God, I'm so sick of this shit, why won't this asshole just leave me the hell alone?" she asked with a mix of fear, anger, and frustration in her eyes.

Raul watched her eyes gloss over. He expected this.

He knew the emotional impact stalking had on its victims. He'd seen it firsthand with his mother, and in the years since, with his clients. Everyone had their breaking point.

The fear of being the target of someone's obsession, not knowing how or why they chose you, or how to make them stop could become unbearable. Many cracked under the psychological strain, even becoming physically ill due to the stress.

So far, Mercedes had been a trooper. Raul knew she was strong, but even those who were strong needed a shoulder to lean on when things got too overwhelming.

He stood, made his way around the table, and pulled Mercedes out of her chair, drawing her in close. She tried to back away, but he wouldn't let her. Eventually, she gave up and let herself be held. She sniffled a few times into his chest as he embraced her.

"I was fifteen when I saw my mother break down under the emotional weight of her stalker."

Mercedes' body stiffened. "Your mom?"

Sighing, Raul pulled back enough to look Mercedes in the eye. "It started when I was fourteen. Random flowers showing up at the door, hang up calls at night." He shook his head. "We had no idea who it was. We changed our number and even stopped the post office from delivering directly to our house. That didn't stop him though. Soon, my mother told my father she felt like she was being followed."

"She told you, too?" Mercedes asked.

Raul shook his head. "They tried to keep it from me. But I saw the change in my mother. She refused to go out after dark. And she and my father often went to a lot of charity events and balls. All of that stopped. She became a recluse."

"Who was it?" Mercedes wanted to know.

"Some guy." He chuckled but there was no humor in it. "After two and a half years, my father was able to hire a PI that was successful in tracking him down. He was a random guy that saw my mom in a grocery store one day. She smiled at him or something, and in his twisted mind, that meant she was in love with him.

"She never even remembered the encounter."

"What happened? Was he arrested?"

Raul nodded. "He was. And then he was let back out. The laws on stalking weren't as advanced back then. My father hired security for my mother. She hated it but knew it was necessary. One day he just stopped. The PI found out that the guy was doing it to someone else and her husband ended up shooting him, killing him."

Mercedes shivered.

Raul wished there was something he could say to make her fear go away. He cupped her face. "I won't let anything happen to you," he whispered into her ear, over and over again.

He held her for a long while. When he felt her body relax, and her sniffles lessen, he pulled back to look down at her. Her eyes were reddened from the tears she shed. He picked up a napkin from the table and dabbed at her cheeks to wipe the tears away, before handing it to her to let her wipe her face and blow her nose.

He tilted her chin to make her look up at him.

"You're safe. Okay? This will be over soon," he promised. It was a promise he was dead set on keeping.

She gave him a shaky smile. "Thank you. I'm so—"

He growled in a warning, halting the apology on her lips.

"Don't you dare apologize. You've been through a lot in the last few months. It's a lot for anybody, and you've handled it better than most."

He palmed her face in his hands and placed a kiss on her forehead.

"I promise you're safe with me. This trip will be everything you expected it to be and more, and when we get home, I will find this person once and for all. And when I do, they will regret the day they ever tried to fuck with you," he said menacingly.

Raul leaned down and took her lips in a powerful kiss that by the end had both of them panting. Mercedes gave him that smile that always brought out his protective instincts.

"Thank you," she whispered.

Stepping back, he pulled Mercedes' chair out for her to sit, before returning to his own seat.

The waiter entered the room a few minutes later and took their orders. While they waited for their meals, Raul continued to reassure Mercedes, telling her of the security detail he hired for this trip, and reminding her that Nikola and Devyn were joining them in a couple of days. He knew she was looking forward to seeing Devyn after spending almost the entire summer apart.

Minutes later the two feasted on almond crusted speckled trout for Mercedes and grilled Angus sirloin for Raul. He managed to bring an upbeat mood to the conversation when he asked about the different sights Mercedes was looking forward to seeing while here.

She smiled and told him that one thing she really wanted to do, that she'd never gotten a chance to do before, was a swamp tour. Raul was game, and made a mental note to check out swamp tours and run them past his security team, right after he assigned his team to get him information on one Stacey Coleman.

Raul was a man who didn't readily believe in coincidences.

He wanted to make sure Stacey Coleman and her aunt were on the up and up, and their surprise run-in was actually a surprise and not planned. Stacey's connection to The Black Kitty gave her access to Mercedes while at the club, and she likely knew of Mercedes' performances around the country.

Raul was nothing if not thorough when it came to doing his job, and he was even more resolute in keeping the woman he loved safe.

Sometime around the time he'd heard Mercedes deliver her speech to the committee members of her school, the small piece of his heart that she didn't already possess, up and fled from his chest and fell right into her hands.

His entire heart and soul was hers. He'd loved women in the past, but nothing like this.

Mercedes was the one for him. Now, he just had to convince her of the same thing, and keep her safe while doing it.

CHAPTER 16

"*D*ev, you look gorgeous!" Mercedes exclaimed as Devyn and Nikola entered their hotel suite. Their friends were staying in the same hotel in another one of the luxury suites. They would only be there for two nights, having just returned from their long stay in Brazil.

They'd left their twin boys with Iris in Atlanta. Devyn was dressed in a pair of teal shorts, paired with an orange, sleeveless top, and a wide, light tan belt that cinched at the waist. She was glowing, and it wasn't just the outfit or her tan, but Mercedes couldn't put her finger on it.

"Thank you, but you are rocking that dress," Devyn returned.

Mercedes herself was dressed in a form-fitting, black and blue summer dress with a peek-a-boo cutout that showed a bit of cleavage. The dress stopped a few inches above the knee, showing off Mercedes' long, toned legs, accentuated by the peep-toe ankle boots with four-inch heels she wore with the dress.

The women embraced as Nikola and Raul greeted one another, and placed kisses on the women's cheeks in greeting. Nikola and Devyn arrived in New Orleans only an hour earlier. That night, the quartet were doing one of the local dinner cruises on the Mississippi

River. Raul's security team had already checked out the cruise to make sure there were no security issues. Before she knew what was happening, Mercedes felt herself being pulled toward the bedroom by Devyn.

"Where are you two going?" Nikola asked both women, but was staring at his wife.

"To the bedroom, we need to catch up. We've got plenty of time before our reservation," Devyn answered over her shoulder. "I'm sure you and Raul want to catch up, too," she finished saying.

"Not really," both men said at the same time, jokingly.

Both Mercedes and Devyn rolled their eyes at the two men.

Once inside of the bedroom, Devyn immediately started with the questions. "So, how are you? Is everything okay?" she asked, worriedly.

The two corresponded via email over the last few weeks. Devyn knew about most of the latest updates regarding Mercedes' stalker, but she still held concern over her friend's well-being.

"I'm fine. I had a mini-breakdown last night, but Raul held me through it." Mercedes sighed, remembering how safe she felt in his arms.

Devyn raised an eyebrow. "A mini-breakdown is to be expected. You've gone through a lot in the last few months. But tell me more about Raul 'holding you through it'."

Mercedes shrugged. "I don't know what to say. I've told you how close we've gotten in the last few months. Shit, the man opened his home up to me. He's sweet and charming, but aggressive at the right moments. I feel safe and cared for when I'm around him.

"Aw hell, I'm starting to sound like you gushing over your hus—" Mercedes stopped short, realizing she was about to compare her relationship with Raul to Devyn and Nikola's.

That couldn't be. Devyn was deeply in love with Nikola, and if it was one thing Mercedes didn't do it was love. She didn't miss the surprised look on Devyn's face.

"Don't even start that shit, Dev," she said, warning her friend.

Devyn threw her hands up defensively. "I didn't say anything. You did all the talking."

"Yeah, but I know what you're thinking, and I want you to cut that out right now."

"Oh really, what am I thinking, then?" Devyn countered.

"You're thinking that over the last two and a half months, I've fallen head-over-heels in love with Raul and it's time to start the wedding planning, but you're wrong. Give up those silly little notions. I mean, yes, he's really smart and charming, and the sex is off the charts hot! Just one look instantly makes my panties wet. He's supportive and encouraging, and underneath all the looks and charm and hell, money, he has one of the biggest hearts of anyone you'll ever meet.

"He seems trustworthy and devoted to family values, which is important to me given my family background, and ..." Mercedes trailed off.

She looked up at Devyn, who wore a smug grin on her face.

"And maybe, just maybe, you more than like him," Devyn finished Mercedes' sentence.

"Shit!" Mercedes exclaimed, falling onto the bed, next to Devyn.

"Look, Little Miss Commitment Phobe, maybe you don't have to figure it all out now. Maybe you can just be honest enough with yourself to admit that you like ... excuse me, *more* than like him, and figure the rest out along the way." Mercedes glanced over at her best friend.

"When the hell did you get so good at giving relationship advice?" she asked flippantly.

Devyn offered a smile. "Since that tall, sexy half-Greek out there made me his. But, even before him, I had a best friend who let me cry on her shoulder through one of the worst break-ups of my life," Devyn said, referring to Mercedes being there for her after her break-up with her emotionally abusive ex.

"I'm just trying to return the favor." Devyn winked and pulled Mercedes in for a hug.

The two women spent a few more minutes catching up, and discussing upcoming plans for the fall. Devyn was planning to start a part-time event-planning business. She told Mercedes all about her plans to drum up business, and how she already had a list of inquiries resulting from her previous work as Andre, Nikola's younger brother's assistant, and having worked on the company's annual Memorial Day Ball.

Mercedes told Devyn about being taken off leave, and the plans she already had for the curriculum for the school year. Mercedes anticipated beginning her planning for the school year as soon as she returned to Atlanta.

"Despite all this with the stalker, you look happy, Cedes," Devyn said, calling Mercedes by her nickname.

Mercedes sighed. "In spite of this crazy person harassing me, I actually am happy." She smiled, realizing how true that statement was.

* * *

"I HAD my team expedite a report on her," Raul told Nikola, as they sat on the couch in the suite's living room. He'd spoken with his team the night before and told Lorenzo to get all the information he could find on Stacey Coleman by the morning. What he found in her file told a bit of a tragic tale, but everything looked on the up and up as far as her being ruled out as Mercedes' stalker.

"And?" Nikola raised his eyebrow, as he leaned back with his arm up on the couch.

"She's not our girl. She's got some history, but everything checks out. Oh, guess what? We know her sister," Raul told Nikola.

Nikola raised an eyebrow in confusion.

"Coleman," Raul said in response to Nikola's silent question. After a few seconds of pondering, realization settled over his features.

"*That* Coleman?" he asked.

Raul nodded. "The one and only. It was buried pretty deep, but my guys found it."

"Small world," Nikola said, raising his glass to his lips.

Raul simply nodded his head in agreement. Both men had previously worked with Stacey's sister while they were in the military. Raul had a few run-ins with her since then through his security firm. Both had an immense amount of respect for the woman.

"Anyway, I still think there's a connection between the club and the stalker. I'm not about to let Mercedes perform there until we find this son of a bitch," Raul said, the mounting frustration evident in his voice.

Nikola didn't miss Raul's emotion. "Well, if you don't think it's safe for Mercedes performing there, I don't want Devyn there either."

Raul looked up at his friend. "Oh yeah? How are you going to convince her not to perform until we catch this person?"

Raul watched as Nikola's lips spread into that silly smile he got when he thought of his wife. "I can be very persuasive when it comes to my wife," Nikola stated, confidently.

"I bet you can be." Raul chuckled and shook his head.

"But you're convinced her stalker is a woman? Are you thinking maybe a performer at the club?" Nikola asked.

"Yeah, the writing in the letters, the break-in and spray paint, all point to someone who's envious of Mercedes. Who wants what she has, and those types of stalkers tend to be the same gender as their victims. So, yeah, I'm convinced it's a woman. She targeted two important aspects of Mercedes' life, her burlesque performing and her career. I feel like now I'm waiting on the other shoe to drop," Raul said contemplatively.

He knew that these types of stalkers targeted important aspects of their victim's lives. Mercedes' stalker went after her as a performer and Mercedes as a career woman. Raul believed their next move would be to target either Mercedes' friends or her family. These stalkers didn't necessarily harm their victims' family and friends, but they would often make threats or bring them into the fold in some way. It was the stalker's way of maintaining control over their victim's lives.

Thinking about Mercedes' family, Raul sighed heavily. She'd talked more about her brother and an aunt of hers than her parents. She told him she wasn't particularly close with her parents because they had rather conservative views.

He'd had his team compose a file on her family. He knew her mother was a dedicated, stay-at-home wife and mother, her brother was a successful accountant at a big accounting firm in Houston, but her father?

Her father was a preacher of a rather large African-American church in the Houston area, but his outside activities didn't often coincide with the messages he delivered from the pulpit. Raul didn't wonder if her father's infidelities had anything to do with Mercedes' fear of commitment, he already knew they did.

Raul and Nikola spent a few more minutes talking about safety concerns before changing the subject to other matters. Raul told Nikola about lunch with his mother a few days earlier, and Nikola shared having spent time with Raul's parents in Rio.

Nikola pulled out his phone to show Raul pictures of the boys from their vacation. Looking at the pictures, Raul realized how much he missed home. It'd only been a few months since his last visit, but he craved the feel of the sand between his toes or hearing the steady rhythm of the waves as they broke along the shoreline in the morning. He longed to bring Mercedes on a trip to his beloved country with him. Raul wanted to see her appreciation for the land he often thought of as magical.

He swiped the phone screen and saw the final picture that showed Nikola, Devyn, and their two boys posing on the beach. Raul's heart lurched in longing to have that. And he wanted it with Mercedes. He looked up to see his best friend staring at him knowingly.

Nikola was gracious enough not to say anything, but he knew that look. It was the one he'd had on his face when he realized the depth of his emotions for Devyn.

A few minutes later, the two women emerged from the bedroom with smiles and ready to go. The couples took a chauffeured vehicle to the dock where they boarded the steamboat that would take them on a two-hour cruise around the Mississippi River with views of the city.

They dined on local seafood, steamed vegetables, and cornbread for the first part of their tour. For the second hour, all four stood to watch, or dance to, the live jazz band that accompanied the tour.

After a lively dance, Raul and Mercedes stepped out on the deck to get some fresh air. He wrapped his arms around her waist, and she leaned back into him, as they swayed to the music that could still be heard from inside. Sweeping the braid Mercedes wore to the side, he placed a gentle kiss on the side of her neck.

She relaxed fully into his embrace and sighed. They spent the remainder of their cruise in that position.

CHAPTER 17

$\mathcal{I}$t was Mercedes' and Raul's third day in New Orleans. They had just seen Nikola and Devyn off, as the couple needed to get back to their boys in Atlanta. Mercedes had performed for the first time the night before. She gave two performances to a packed audience, which included Devyn and Nikola, and of course Raul keeping a constant watch on the side of the stage.

The entire night had gone off without a hitch, and when she headed backstage her friends applauded and congratulated her on a performance well done. Mercedes was elated at the turn out. She was even more overjoyed at having Raul there to share it with. He was more than just a bodyguard, or the man she was fucking regularly.

Everything she'd told Devyn the day before was right. He had all the qualities most women would find appealing in a partner, and he had a way of making her feel as if she was the most important person in the room.

Was it love?

Mercedes couldn't know for sure. It had only been a few weeks they'd been together. *It's too soon to tell if I'm in love*, she thought. Or maybe she was just denying the inevitable. Either way, she knew when she was in his arms it felt right.

For now, that was good enough.

On this third day in New Orleans, Mercedes did not have to perform. Raul had set up the reservations for the swamp tour. They spent the day out touring the swamp around New Orleans, watching alligators emerge as the tour guides encouraged them out of the water with food, and seeing the different types of wildlife that resided in the marsh.

Once the tour ended, the pair strolled the streets of the French Quarter, stopping for lunch of crab cakes and corn on the cob followed by freshly prepared beignets. Later in the day they did one of the Voodoo tours, where topics such as the Haitian Rebellions, Slavery, and the Code Noir in Colonial New Orleans were covered.

Raul mentioned to Mercedes how much of New Orleans culture and history reminded him of Brazil's history and different cultures. As the tour ended, he told Mercedes about Candomble, a Brazilian religion that emerged out of slavery and was a combination of West African religions. Many of the beliefs and traditions of the religion mirrored that of New Orleans Voodoo, which also was born out of West African religions and beliefs.

Once they reached their hotel, the couple opted to shower and order room service for dinner.

An hour later, Mercedes emerged from the bathroom to find the room lit by numerous candles spread throughout the bedroom and living room area. The floor was sprinkled with rose petals, as was the bed. Mercedes smiled when she heard the light sounds of Carl Thomas' "Emotional" floating through the air. And in the middle of it all, stood a barefoot Raul dressed in a pair of dark jeans and a V-neck.

"What is this?" she asked.

"This is dinner." He came over to her and placed a light kiss on her cheek. "Finish getting dressed and meet me in the other room for dinner," he ordered, moving away from her. "I already picked out your outfit … it's on the bed. It's for easy access." He turned and walked into the living room.

On the bed lay one of Mercedes' strapless summer dresses and nothing else.

Easy access indeed, she thought as she removed her robe, quickly moisturized her skin, and slipped into the purple dress.

She put her hair in a loose chignon, then made her way into the living room. The furniture had been rearranged to make space for the table the waiter brought up. In the center of the circular table sat a bottle of champagne chilling in ice.

Raul had ordered the chicken breast for himself and vegetable risotto for Mercedes. She walked toward Raul, who held a glass of champagne out to her.

"A toast," he said, once she took the glass.

"What are we toasting?"

He smiled that mischievous smile.

"To a great performance last night, a great one tomorrow, and a very fun night tonight," he said as he clinked his glass to hers.

After finishing their glasses, Raul placed them on the table, pulled out the chair for Mercedes, and then seated himself. They ate and talked about Mercedes' performance the following night. She'd considered paying tribute to her idol, Josephine Baker, by doing a rendition of her famous banana skirt dance, but that felt too contrived because it'd been done so many times before.

"Instead, I'm thinking of doing my Elizabeth 'China Doll' Dickerson routine," she told him.

Raul lifted an eyebrow and shook his head. "Is this a new set?"

"Not really, but I haven't performed it a ton. It's fun because I pin balloons to my costume and then allow the audience members to pop one balloon at a time. With each pop, one piece of my costume falls away."

Mercedes paused when the expression on Raul's face turned serious.

"This set would have you venturing out into the audience?" His tone had hardened from just a minute ago.

"It would," Mercedes said slowly, realizing that couldn't happen, for obvious reasons.

"Then I suggest you find another set to perform." Raul's comment brokered no argument.

However right he might be, Mercedes still bristled at the tone in his voice. "Or, how about I suggest you not tell me how to perform. That's my arena. Security is yours."

He narrowed his eyes. "Don't, Mercedes. You know damn well having you go out into the audience is a safety risk we cannot afford to take."

She gave a casual shrug. "I'm sure your security team could figure it out. I'm doing the set."

"The hell you are. Don't make me repeat myself."

Mercedes' nipples pebbled at the growl in his voice. Too turned on, she let her façade slip as she bit her bottom lip.

Raul groaned. "You were fucking with me," he realized.

Mercedes let out a laugh. "I'm not an idiot."

"We're done with dinner." Raul abruptly stood. He fought like hell to remember the plan for their night that he'd put in place because everything in his body wanted to take Mercedes right on the dinner table.

Instead, he moved to the small speaker that played music from his laptop, turned up the music, and returned to Mercedes, extending his hands toward her.

"Dance with me," he commanded.

Mercedes allowed herself to be guided away from the table and pulled in his embrace. Raul brought her in tight to his body, allowing her to feel his level of arousal against her stomach. Mercedes' breath hitched.

They swayed to the rhythm of the music for a little while before Raul pulled back.

"You're so beautiful," he said, looking at her with such desire in his eyes that it made Mercedes shiver. He pulled her close, taking her lips in a kiss filled with everything he wanted to say to her.

Mercedes pressed herself deeper into Raul as his lips continued to take possession of her. Raul walked Mercedes back to their bedroom, stopping at the edge of the bed. He moved back slightly, his lips hovering over hers.

"Do you trust me?" he asked above a whisper.

Mercedes, still reeling from the kiss, was confused.

"What?" she asked breathlessly, wanting to feel his lips on hers again.

"Do you trust me?" he repeated

Mercedes searched his eyes for what he was really asking. She could see that her answer mattered a great deal to him. She nodded.

"Yes, I trust you," she said softly, meaning it.

Raul brought her in for another kiss, and moved his hand behind his back, pulling out a blindfold he'd tucked into his back pocket.

"Close your eyes," he directed.

Mercedes complied, and then gasped when she felt the blindfold cover her eyes, but she didn't pull away. Raul secured the blindfold around the back of her head—not too tight, but enough to know that it wouldn't easily come undone. He placed kisses on Mercedes' forehead, nose, and mouth, moving down to her neck and shoulders. He allowed his hands to gather the ends of her dress so he could access her soft thighs.

Raul caressed her thighs before moving around to palm her ass cheeks.

"Mmmm," Mercedes moaned, when he bit her earlobe.

He moved back to her mouth, absorbing the end of her moan in his. He let one hand trail back around to her front and graze over the hood of her pussy. Mercedes automatically parted her legs to grant him access, but Raul was not ready to go there yet.

He moved his hands to the top of her dress, and slowly pulled it down, letting it pool at her feet. He picked Mercedes up in his arms and moved to the side of the bed, kneeling down to place her in the middle. Grabbing her arms overhead, he straddled her naked body before leaning down and whispering in her ear.

"They say that when blindfolded your other senses are heightened. Your sense of hearing is increased. Sense of touch is more magnified. Even taste is more intense. You'll have to let me know if they're right. Don't move, querida. Stay just like this," he said before rolling off the bed.

* * *

MERCEDES' body hummed with excitement and arousal. Her core temperature lowered when Raul moved from the bed. She felt the softness of the rose petals that lay under her body. She tried to figure out where Raul was, then she heard his feet padding along the carpeted floor.

A few seconds later, the music volume increased. She recognized the opening lines of Kelly Rowland's "Motivation".

Mercedes gasped when she felt the tip of a rose petal brush along the underside of her foot. The petal was run up her legs, the inside of her thighs, up her stomach, where the softness of Raul's lips kissed her belly button, before he stuck his tongue inside.

Wetness instantly pooled between her legs.

Her belly button was a particularly erogenous zone for her. He placed kisses up her stomach, before encircling a nipple with his mouth and letting his hand play with the other. Mercedes' skin warmed from the skin-to-skin contact, and she knew he was completely naked when she his stiff cock pressed in between her thighs.

"Mmmm, Raul," she cooed when he nipped her nipple and allowed his thumb to make small circles on her clit.

Before she became too lost in what he was doing, she once again felt the absence of his warmth as he moved from above her. She almost called out in frustration, but bit her lip instead.

The ending words of the song played as if foreshadowing Raul's intent for the rest of their night. Mercedes knew he'd chosen that song on purpose. Her body burned … ached to be touched. To touch of his hands all over her.

She, once again, felt the bed dip.

"Aaahhh," she cried out, as a freezing cold and wet substance circle her nipple

"Ice to cool you off, querida." Raul's voice was thick with desire. He circled her second nipple with the ice before dragging it down her body. Raul crawled down her body and allowed the ice to melt, stopping to lick along the way.

Mercedes thought the ice had completely melted when she only felt his kisses on her belly and his hands part her thighs.

Raul's weight shifted and he positioned himself between her legs.

"Aaahhhhh," she cried out again and arched her back off the bed, feeling the chilling cold sensation of the ice on her pussy lips.

"R-Raul pl-please," she moaned in a strained voice, as his mouth dragged the ice up to her clit, circling it.

Raul used his tongue and lips to push the ice cube in and out of her until it melted completely. He tortured her in the most splendid way.

Mercedes' thrashed her head against the pillows, begging for Raul to end her torment and to take her. She screamed out her orgasm.

Satisfied, Raul rose to his knees and untied the blindfold. Taking a few moments to let her eyes adjust to seeing again, she blinked looking up to see Raul hovering over her.

"Et te adoro," he whispered, as she felt him ease his cock inside of her.

As soon as Raul's cock was lodged deep inside of her core, Mercedes turned the tables on him. Moving quickly, she reversed their positions, so she was straddling him. She smiled sexily at the surprised look on his face.

When Mercedes raised her hips and moved down, slowly impaling herself on him, Raul's expression changed from one of shock to pure ecstasy. She knew he loved when she was on top. Raul's hands reached around to firmly grip Mercedes' ass, spurring her on. She bounced on his cock in a rhythm that drove them both wild with passion.

Rising slowly then swiveling her hips as she descended, Mercedes threw her head back when the tip of his cock pressed against her G-spot. Raul's hands gripped her ass even tighter, as he raised his hips to meet Mercedes'.

"Ohh shit, Raul. Fuck," she panted, planting her hands on his chest. Mercedes looked down into Raul's eyes and saw lust, passion, and another emotion she was too scared to name.

As soon as their eyes made contact, Raul needed to be closer to her. Sitting up so he was seated on the bed, he wrapped Mercedes' legs around his back and pulled her head down for another scorching kiss.

Mercedes pumped her hips on Raul's cock as his tongue made love to her mouth. He moved his hand around and pressed his thumb to Mercedes' clit, massaging in the same rhythm his tongue was stroking her mouth. Within minutes Mercedes pulled from Raul's mouth and buried her head in his neck as her orgasm loomed. She could feel an intense orgasm coming, and her hips continued to move as if they had a mind of their own.

"Rauul, I'm commmming," she yelled out.

The squeeze of Mercedes' pussy walls on Raul's cock sent him over the edge right behind her.

"Eu te amo, querida!" Raul yelled as he came.

Mercedes held Raul close as he came.

They remained in that seated position for long moments, both overwhelmed by the intensity of their lovemaking. Mercedes let her head rest in the crook of Raul's neck while he stroked his hand up and down her back in a soothing motion. When they both caught their breaths, Raul moved, turning to deposit Mercedes on the bed and pull himself out of her.

On shaky legs, he rose from the bed and went to the bathroom, throwing away the used condom, and retrieving a warm cloth to wipe Mercedes and then himself down. Climbing back into the bed, he pulled a half-sleep Mercedes into his arms.

She snuggled closer into his warmth.

"They were right. The senses are so much more intense when blindfolded," she said around a yawn.

Raul chuckled. "Tired you out, huh?" he asked cockily.

"Don't worry, I'll be ready to go again after some rest." She snuggled deeper into his embrace.

"I'm counting on it, querida," he said before Mercedes fell into a deep sleep.

Raul laid awake for a while longer, just holding Mercedes and listening to her breathing. He'd been shocked at what he yelled to Mercedes in the middle of making love to her. He'd told her he loved her in Portuguese, and he didn't regret it. He didn't know if she was ready to hear the words in English, but she'd better be ready soon because he had no intentions of letting this woman go.

CHAPTER 18

"Ten minutes, Dahlia," Jazzy, the stage kitten at the New Orleans club Mercedes was performing at, came to tell her.

Mercedes was backstage with Raul in one of the single dressing rooms.

"Thank you." She smiled her gratitude and continued to make sure all the balloons were fastened in place.

"How do I look?" she asked Raul.

"Like you should let me take you back to the hotel so we can have a replay of last night ... and this morning," he said seductively.

Mercedes was wearing a pair of fishnets, a pair of black lace panties with pink ruffling at the back, and a black corset embroidered with pink rhinestones. She'd strategically tied six balloons around her corset and panties. Each time she popped one of the balloons, a piece of her corset came undone. The last balloon would be the one to reveal her nude, except for the pink heart pasties she wore.

She winked at Raul. "After my performance," she purred. "Right now, it's showtime!" She clapped excitedly.

Raul laughed and turned to head out the door. Mercedes dutifully followed. When they reached the stage, she felt energized seeing the crowd. This was the culminating event of the summer. She was pumped to get on stage, and as she looked to her right, she knew Raul's presence made it even more special.

"Coming to the stage all the way from Atlanta, Black Dahliaaaaa! Give it up for her, ladies and gentlemen!" the announcer bellowed into the microphone before exiting the stage.

The music of Janelle Monae's "Q.U.E.E.N." began playing as Mercedes stepped on stage, shimmying across. She swayed and stepped in time to the music, pumping up the crowd as she dipped, shaking her shoulders, allowing her cleavage to be seen by those in the front row.

Mercedes danced as she felt the power of the words of the song. She'd chosen the song because it spoke to her questions about sexuality and religion. Questions she'd had seeing her father, a supposedly devout preacher, admonish her for her budding sexuality as an adolescent, while he cheated on his wife.

Mercedes popped the first balloon, and the bottom of her corset came undone. She heard the roar of the crowd as they noticed her corset coming undone. She teased them some as she dropped to her knees and wiggled her hips, popping another balloon. Raucous cheers from the crowd erupted as they delighted in the sight of Mercedes slowly revealing her body from behind the corset.

Minutes later, Mercedes was down to her last balloon. As the final words of Janelle Monae's song played, Mercedes popped the balloon. A cloud of purple glitter burst from the balloon, and when it cleared, Mercedes remained in her panties and pasties, giving the crowd one more shimmy before she fled the stage. The audience members whooped and stomped their feet in admiration.

"Perfeito, querida!" Raul gushed as Mercedes walked into his arms after exiting the stage.

Perfect.

And that's exactly how she felt around him, as if she was perfect. Nothing wrong with her.

She savored the feel of his embrace and laughed when she pulled back to find him covered in purple glitter just like her. His good-natured laughter warmed her soul.

Together they walked back to her dressing room, but their elation was short-lived.

* * *

"Boss, we have an issue," Lorenzo said just above a whisper close to Raul's ear so Mercedes wouldn't overhear. It'd been thirty minutes or so after Mercedes' performance and they were in her dressing room.

Raul couldn't tell Mercedes enough how excellent she was on stage.

For her part, Mercedes was on cloud nine. She'd enjoyed the last few days, and her performances in New Orleans. She'd told Raul she had never enjoyed the city like this until visiting with him. As she dressed, the couple discussed their plans to go out to dinner with Stacey and her aunt that evening. They'd spotted the pair eating breakfast that morning, and they stopped to say hello.

Stacey and her aunt invited the two to dinner, before they both departed on their respective flights in the morning. As Mercedes talked about her performance and cleaning up the remnants of the glitter, there was a knock on the door.

Now Lorenzo was telling Raul there was an issue. Raul stepped outside, closing the door behind him.

"What is it?"

"Dwayne and Linda Holmes are here, and they are demanding to see Mercedes."

Raul froze. Dwayne and Linda Holmes were Mercedes' parents.

What were they doing here?

"Are you sure it's them?" Raul asked, wanting to play it safe.

"Yup, it's them. I verified myself with my own eyes. They said they'd received a letter a few days ago telling them that Mercedes was performing here. The person sent them tickets to her performance and a note attached," Lorenzo confirmed.

"What'd it say?" Raul asked.

"See for yourself." Lorenzo pulled out the note he'd gotten from Mercedes' parents.

The note read: **Is this the daughter you raised?** It had a half-naked Mercedes performing on stage at The Black Kitty.

"Damn it," Raul muttered under his breath. He knew this was the work of Mercedes' stalker. He would do anything to preserve Mercedes' good mood, but that didn't seem possible. He knew her parents wouldn't be happy with what they'd witnessed on stage.

"Give me a minute," Raul told Lorenzo, before opening the door to the dressing room. Stepping inside, he saw Mercedes was now dressed in a sleeveless floral romper, with her hair falling in curls around her shoulders. She looked beautiful as she smiled and turned toward him.

"This glitter is going to be a bitch to get out." She laughed, but having obviously noticed the somber expression on Raul's face she stopped. "What's wrong?"

"Querida, there are some guests from the performance who want to talk with you," Raul stated cautiously.

"Guests?"

"Yes, they were in the audience and saw your performance."

"I don't understand."

As a safety precaution, Raul did not let anyone visit her in the dressing room. He could tell she didn't understand why he was mentioning this to her.

"It's your parents," he said finally. He saw the look on Mercedes' face change from one of confusion to shock to fear in a manner of seconds.

"My parents? H-How do you know?" she asked.

Raul sighed. "I looked up your parents, just to make sure everything was on the up and up with them. My team knows your whole family. This person stalking you sent tickets of your performance to them a few days ago along with a picture of you mid-performance," he told her.

Mercedes slumped back against the wall. Just like that, her good mood was deflated. She wrapped her arms around her waist in an effort to guard her emotions. Raul's heart ached seeing her upset.

"I can send them away. You don't have to see them," he consoled, taking a step toward her. He reached around her waist and pulled her close to him. "Querida, I know you don't have the best relationship with your parents. If you want me to, just say the word, and I can have them escorted out of here and all the way back to Houston."

Raul wanted her to say yes. To give him the green light to get rid of her parents, at least for now, and they could forget this incident ever happened. They'd enjoy their final night in New Orleans and deal with everything else later. But he also knew she wouldn't.

"I can't do that." Mercedes inhaled deeply. "I've hidden this part of my life from them for too long. I'm a big girl. I can take whatever they have to say." Standing, she squared her shoulders.

Raul's heart swelled with the same pride he had when he saw her defend herself in front of her school's committee. "Okay, I'll have them escorted in."

Raul stepped out and told Lorenzo it was okay to bring her parents back. He could see the tension in Mercedes' body when he returned to the room.

* * *

"It'll be okay, querida," Raul told her as he massaged both of her shoulders.

She gave him a faint smile of gratitude.

About ten minutes later there was a knock on the door.

Time to face the music, Mercedes thought as she watched Raul pull the door open.

There stood both of her parents. The crinkle in her father's forehead and his downturned lips told the story of his ire. Behind her father was Mercedes' mother, biting her lower lip and gripping the strap of her handbag tightly. She observed their body language.

Where Mercedes' father was clearly angry, her mother appeared to be nervous and fidgety. When Mercedes' father started to head toward her, Raul moved to block his path. The older man paused, looking up at Raul.

"Mr. and Mrs. Holmes, I'm Raul Santiago, a friend of Mercedes," he introduced himself by holding out his hand, but Mercedes' father was in no mood for introductions.

He looked over Raul's shoulder.

"Mercedes Patrice Holmes," her father said in the disciplinary tone he used on her as a child.

Mercedes took a step forward and placed a hand on Raul's shoulder. "It's okay, Raul."

His body relaxed ever so slightly, and he moved to the side, closing the door. He turned and stood with his arms at his side, ready to jump in just in case.

Her father turned to Raul. "Young man, I am sure you are needed elsewhere."

"I'm fine right here," Raul said flatly and folded his arms across his chest.

"Dad, Mom, it's okay. Raul is my friend," she said, wanting to say he was more than a friend.

When her father turned back to her she nearly flinched at the disgusted look on his face.

"A friend?" he asked mockingly. "A friend who lets you get on stage and whore yourself for hundreds of people? What type of friend is that?" her father roared.

Raul took a menacing step toward Mercedes' father, but was cut off by Mercedes' mother.

"Dwayne, please. We can talk calmly about this," her mother tried to reason.

"Calmly? Calmly? Linda, did you see what I saw? Our daughter on stage shaking her naked tail for hundreds of people? This is not the woman I raised. I don't know where you went wrong, but this will end today!" he roared.

"No," Mercedes said more calmly than she felt. "I'm not giving up performing. I'm sorry you had to find out this way, but it's not something I am ashamed of, nor should I be."

For a brief second, her father looked taken aback. Throughout her life, the one person Mercedes had not spoken back to was her father. She spent years regaining the voice she felt she'd lost in her childhood. She had no problem speaking her mind to others, and now it was her turn to tell her father exactly how she felt.

"You shouldn't be ashamed? You shouldn't be ashamed to get on stage and take your clothes off like some common hooker on the street? I spent years teaching you right from wrong. Years telling you to keep your damn legs closed and now here you are acting like some hoe from the hood.

"I knew you were fast growing up. I knew it, and now look at you. You think that man," he pointed to Raul, "respects you? No! He only wants what's between your legs. That's clearly all you're good for, what's between your legs! Did you even think of what the people in my congregation would say about this? You're selfish, that's what you are, a selfish little girl!" Mercedes' father yelled.

Mercedes heart ached from the sting of his words, but instead of reeling in the shame or guilt like she did as a child, she felt something else. This time, her body started to burn with fury. How dare he talk to her about being a whore when he'd been cheating on his wife for years? Out of the corner of her eye, Mercedes saw Raul take another step toward her father, but she gave him a look to let him know she was okay.

She needed to have her say, here and now.

"Did you ever think about your congregation?" she asked.

"What?" her father yelled.

"Did you ever think about your congregation? All those times you were stepping out on Mama. All those nights we waited for you to come home for dinner, food getting cold on the table."

"Mercedes!" She heard her mother gasp, but she was just getting started.

Mercedes took delight in seeing the shocked expression on her father's face.

"What's the matter, Dad? Don't like being confronted with your own dirt? My whole life you've been telling me only fast women do this or whores do that, right before you went out and bedded those same women you trashed.

"I'm a grown ass woman, and I have not lived under your roof in a while. I no longer live by your rules. I am a burlesque dancer and I have been for years. And while we're at it, you should know that I am far from a virgin, and I've also dated plenty of women and men. You see," she said, taking a step toward her father, "unlike you, I don't preach one thing and practice another. I am who I am, and I have no more secrets. Can you say the same?" she challenged, looking her father square in the eye.

Mercedes could see her father's fury boiling over. Not only his fury, but the shock and incredulity of having his own indiscretions thrown in his face, by his daughter no less. She knew exactly when he'd made the decision to strike her.

She saw the look in his eyes, even before his hand moved. She braced herself for the hit, turning her head, but it never came.

Raul was much quicker than her father.

Obviously he had seen the change in Dwayne's body language and his instincts kicked in. Moving swiftly, Raul grabbed Dwayne's hand, spinning him around, and slamming him against the wall. Both Mercedes and her mother gasped.

Raul's nostrils flared, knuckles turning white from gripping Dwayne's wrist and neck so tightly. Mercedes could see Raul was barely able to contain his anger.

"You just said some terrible shit to your own daughter, but I held off snatching you up for her sake. But it'll be a cold day in hell before I stand by and let a man put his hands on a woman, especially my woman," Raul's voice came out low but full of deadly promise.

Raul's grip tightened on the older man's wrist and throat. He heavily contemplated taking the man outside and showing him exactly what real hurt was all about. At that moment, it didn't matter to Raul who this man was to Mercedes.

All he saw was a man who'd hurt his woman.

"Raul, please." He felt Mercedes put her hand on his arm.

Raul moved in closer to Dwayne's ear. "The only reason I'm

letting you walk out of here right now is to prevent your daughter and your wife any more grief. Next time you won't be so lucky." Raul eased back slowly, giving the man one last deadly look before releasing him.

Dwayne hunched over, gasping for air, but Raul had no sympathy.

"Mercedes, this isn't … this," her mother stumbled trying to find the words to fix this situation.

"I'm sorry, Mama. I think you both should go," Mercedes said.

A look of complete sadness came over Mercedes' mother's face. Mercedes' heartstrings tugged. The last thing she wanted to do was hurt her mother. She knew bringing up her father's affair was also hurtful to her mother, but she couldn't abide by his double standards any longer.

Linda finally nodded and turned to her husband who was now standing with his hand around his neck, massaging it. Mercedes gave her parents one last look before turning away from them. In a way she felt relieved that they knew the truth. She wouldn't beg for their forgiveness, and she was at the point now where she believed it was her parents—especially her father—who needed to ask for forgiveness.

Mercedes watched as Raul walked out of the door and whispered into the ear of one of his employees before returning to her.

"I'm so sorry, querida. Are you okay?" he asked, reaching out to massage her shoulders.

Mercedes nodded.

"We can cancel our plans for tonight or even head back to Atlanta if you're not up for it," he suggested.

Mercedes thought about it for a few moments. Before seeing her parents, she was really looking forward to spending their final night in New Orleans, going out with Stacey and her aunt, and one final night with Raul away from Atlanta.

Once she got back, she knew she'd have to start thinking about the upcoming school year. She wasn't ready to let go just yet. She stood up straight and squared her shoulders, shaking off her somber mood from seeing her parents and arguing with her father.

"No, I want to stay. We only have one night left here. Let's not waste it." She gave him a half smile.

"You sure?"

Mercedes nodded.

"Then we'll stay." He pulled her in for a kiss on her forehead and a hug.

Leaning into Raul, Mercedes breathed deeply. She found strength in leaning on him. When she felt him wrap his strong arms around her, she let her head fall to his shoulder. They stood there, arms wrapped around one another for a while, Raul's embrace giving her strength, and reassuring her that everything was okay.

Whoever this stalker was, was trying to weaken her, trying to take everything from her, one by one. Instead, they were doing the opposite, making her confront the parts of her life she'd been trying to keep separated since she'd moved out of her parents' home.

She no longer had any secrets to hide. She wasn't ashamed of who she was, and she would not let anyone shame her. While this stalker had made her confront these issues, she knew it was the man who held her, that gave her the strength to endure it all. She picked her head up and looked into his eyes.

Mercedes saw so many emotions swimming in those deep brown pools. She found comfort in knowing he didn't attempt to hide his feelings for her. They were right there on display for her to see. This incredibly handsome, strong, accomplished man who could have just about anyone he wanted, wasn't backing out at the first sign of trouble or family strife.

It made Mercedes want to be brave too. She leaned up and kissed him.

"Thank you," she whispered against his lips. At his confused expression, instead of explaining she kissed him again. She'd known long ago that Raul wasn't just some fling she was having.

CHAPTER 19

*R*aul looked up when he heard a knock at his door.

"Hey, boss. You got a minute? I think I found some-thing you may want to hear." Matt, one of his top forensics guys, stood at his door.

"You have something for me on Mercedes' stalker?" Raul asked.

Raul and Mercedes had returned from New Orleans two days before, and he'd given directives to a number of his staff members to turn up the heat in searching for Mercedes' stalker. She was supposed to return to school the following day to begin organizing the teachers and training for the school year that would be starting the following week.

Once the school year was back in session, Mercedes couldn't remain secluded in his home, in between trips to her performances. She had to get back to her normal life, and Raul was determined to make sure this person would not be able to do any more harm than they already had done.

"Yeah, boss. So, as you know we started going over all the records for everyone who works at The Black Kitty. Interesting name for a club, by the way," Matt said, looking at Raul.

When Raul merely stared at him, Matt cleared his throat and

continued, "Right. So anyway, we decided to dig a little deeper into the employees at The Black Kitty. This time around we did much more extensive checks and almost everyone checked out."

This was when Raul's ears perked up. Standing, he came around the front of his desk, to park himself in front of where Matt was now sitting. Raul leaned back on his desk, giving Matt his undivided attention.

"Who didn't?" Raul asked.

"Well, you know the one they call a … uh, stage kitten, her stage name is Roxxy? Yeah, well, the name she claims as hers is Roxanne Summers, but that name and social security number didn't exist before 2007, and I … well, *we* know she's not an eight-year-old child.

"Of course that got my attention, so I went back to do a fingerprint analysis. Lorenzo was able to swipe one of Mercedes' gloves that Roxxy brought back to her room after a performance. Do you know how hard it is to retrieve fingerprints from clothing? It's not easy at all. First you have to—"

"Matt," Raul interrupted sternly. "Get back to what it was you found," Raul commanded brusquely.

"Right, sorry. I was able to pull a partial thumbprint from Mercedes' glove; one that did not belong to Mercedes. We searched the national database, and found there was a hit, but the records were sealed. Apparently, this person was a minor when the crime occurred. Anyway, after getting one of the hackers here to do their thing, we were able to get into the records. Turns out, Roxanne Summers' real name is Rochelle Roberts and guess where she grew up?" Matt asked confidently.

"Chicago."

Raul knew that was the answer because the hacker they'd found who'd tried to break into the hotel security system was based in Chicago, and he'd been the one who was paid to set up a fake online dating page to lure in the man, who was hired to rush the stage at The Black Kitty.

The hacker was also paid to get addresses on Mercedes' employer and the parents of her students. Lorenzo tracked the hacker down in Chicago, and his story was that a friend of a friend had hired him.

He'd never met the woman Matt was referring to.

"Yup," Matt said, nodding his head enthusiastically. "But that's not all. Guess where she was born?"

Raul had a feeling he knew, but waited for Matt to answer his own question.

"Houston. She was born to one Thomasina Roberts. Father's name was not on the birth certificate. Thomasina lived with her young daughter, Rochelle, in the Houston area until she was about two, before moving to Chicago."

Raul's mind immediately began conjuring up all sorts of questions. What was Rochelle's connection to Mercedes? Did their family have some sort of connection? Why was Rochelle signaling Mercedes out?

By now, Raul was sure that Rochelle was Mercedes' stalker. She'd been working at The Black Kitty for close to a year now, and within months of her working there, was when Mercedes began receiving the hang-up calls, then the break-in and ensuing forms of harassment.

What was it about Mercedes' that triggered this Rochelle? Raul felt it was deeper than just jealousy over Mercedes' performances.

He had the feeling Rochelle deliberately sought out The Black Kitty to work at because she knew Mercedes was a regular there.

"I need you to get me everything you can find on this Rochelle and fast," Raul ordered.

Matt nodded. "Will do, boss. For now, here's some interesting reading material from the preliminary information I've got so far."

Raul took the folder Matt offered him and opened it. The first sheet was an image of Rochelle from the club, followed by an image of her mug shot when she was arrested at the age of fourteen. She had been arrested for shoplifting. Raul thumbed through the file before coming back to the first picture. The image struck him for some reason.

She looked … familiar.

Matt stood to leave, as Raul continued to stare at the picture. He knew there was something there, but he couldn't put his finger on it. A few seconds later it clicked.

"Matt," he called just as Matt reached the door. "Work with Lorenzo and get me everything you can find on Rochelle's mother. I want to know all about Thomasina's background and history in Houston. Get me anything you can find on who Rochelle's father might be. And I need it yesterday. Understood?"

"Got it, boss," Matt said before turning and hurrying out the door to do Raul's bidding.

When Matt left, Raul rounded his desk in search of his cell phone. He knew Mercedes had gone over to Nikola and Devyn's to have brunch with Devyn and the boys.

He felt safe knowing she wasn't alone. Nikola's home, like his, was in a gated community and just as secure. Still, he wanted to check on her, though he wouldn't tell her what he'd just discovered until he was absolutely sure.

He decided to just send a text checking in.

* * *

"Hmmmm."

Mercedes looked up from her phone to see Devyn staring at her with laughter in her eyes. "Hmmmm, what?" Mercedes snapped.

"Nothing," Devyn said, smiling as she took a sip of her orange juice.

The two women sat on Devyn's back patio. They had just put Devyn's boys down for their mid-morning nap. Now, they ate a hearty brunch prepared by Devyn and Nikola's chef, consisting of eggs, potato latkes, bacon, cut up fruit and orange juice.

"Don't you dare nothing me, chick. What was all that about?" Mercedes insisted.

Devyn laughed. "Calm down. I can tell it was Raul by the way you were all smiling and giddy looking at your phone."

Mercedes couldn't fully deny Devyn's words. She was happy whenever Raul took the time out of his day to check in on her.

"Did you call me giddy? See, you're doing too much. Happy? Yes. Giddy? Not so much," Mercedes retorted, trying to preserve some of the air of coolness she had when it came to relationships.

"Oh please. Try that on someone else who doesn't know you. You were downright delirious with happiness responding to that text. I should have taken a picture for all those times you made fun of me when Nikola and I were dating," Devyn teased.

"Girl, whatever. That's 'cause you were damn near drooling over that man whenever you heard his name. Hell, you still do." Mercedes laughed.

"Yeah, well, you need to check your bottom lips because I think I see some drool there," Devyn countered.

"Don't make me fight you," Mercedes said, tossing her napkin at Devyn.

"You could, but you wouldn't want to hurt your next goddaughter or son, would you?"

Mercedes paused, absorbing what Devyn just revealed. She gasped in excitement. "You heffa! I knew it!" she yelled, standing to give her friend a big hug. She was just as excited as the first time she learned Devyn was pregnant.

"I should have known when I saw the bacon on the table," Mercedes said, remembering Devyn's first pregnancy when she craved bacon, a food she rarely ate.

Devyn laughed.

"How far along are you? How long have you known? Did you tell Nikola yet? I bet he's excited," Mercedes rambled off her questions.

For the next hour or so, Devyn and Mercedes talked about the pregnancy. Devyn and Nikola had found out while they vacationed in Brazil. She was about ten weeks along, and of course, Mercedes was going to be the godmother again.

Mercedes was truly happy for her friend, and for the first time she found herself wondering what it would be like to be pregnant. When she thought of the person she would want to be the father of her children, one face came to mind. The familiar, handsome face with golden skin and warm, brown eyes filled her head.

Mercedes' phone rang as she got in her car to leave Devyn's home. Raul's house was only about a ten-minute drive from Devyn and Nikola's home. She looked down at her phone to see it was Ron Sherman calling. She assumed it had something to do with the following day's training.

"Hi, Ron."

"H-Hi, Mercedes," he responded, clearing his throat. "Do you have a minute?"

"Yeah, I'm just leaving a friend's house. Did you need something?"

"Yes, I need you to come down to the school. We have to go over the agenda for tomorrow and I may need you to help me sort through some files before everyone else gets here," he stated.

Mercedes figured this was about the new student files they received every year prior to the start of the school semester.

"Uh, okay, Ron. Are you at school now?" Mercedes asked, glancing at her watch.

"Yes, can you meet me here in twenty minutes? It shouldn't take too long," he assured her.

"Okay, I'm a little farther out so I should be there within the next thirty minutes," she said before hanging up.

* * *

MERCEDES WASN'T aware that Ron hung up the phone and stared directly into the business end of a 9mm.

"Nice job, Sherman. You may make it out of this alive after all. Unlike your assistant principal."

Ron stared at the woman who had a crazed gleam in her eye.

He knew this day would not end well for Mercedes if this woman had her way. He silently prayed they both made it out alive.

CHAPTER 20

"Okay, boss, we've been working nonstop and found a little more information," Lorenzo said as Raul exited the conference room in his office. He'd been in a meeting with a high-level client on some important security issues his business had been having.

Raul told his team that he wanted more information on Thomasina and Rochelle Roberts once he finished his meeting. Lorenzo was waiting for him at the door.

"Tell me what you got," Raul said as he strode down the hallway to his office.

"Thomasina was born and raised in Houston's 3rd Ward. From the looks of it, her family was pretty much working class. Her father was a mechanic, and her mother was a preschool teacher. She was raised in the church. As she got older, she graduated from the local high school, and attended community college. It's still fuzzy on who could be Rochelle's father, but we found an original copy of her birth certificate. There was a father's name placed on the certificate," Lorenzo said as he pulled out a picture of an old birth certificate.

The image was blurry, but Raul was able to make out the name of the father. He stood there stunned.

Dwayne Holmes.

It all began to come together, as Lorenzo told him more about Rochelle's childhood.

"Apparently, she had it pretty rough after moving to Chicago," Lorenzo continued. "Her mother fell ill with Multiple Sclerosis, and she spent a large portion of her childhood caring for her mother instead of being a kid. Turns out, she was caught shoplifting to get clothes for school and to make a little extra money to support herself and her mother. She was arrested, but was let off easy. Since then, she stayed out of trouble, as far as law enforcement knows.

"Rochelle finally had to put her mother in a home about eighteen months ago, and within a few months, Thomasina suffered a stroke. She died as a result of the stroke."

Raul knew this was the woman. He knew he was reading the file of the woman who'd been targeting Mercedes. It must have been the death of her mother that triggered her. He still had questions as to why she fixated on Mercedes, but he fully intended to ask Rochelle those questions.

"What's her current address?" he barked out the question to Lorenzo.

"Here it is. She's been leasing a month-to-month apartment in the same complex as Mercedes."

At that moment, Raul was so grateful he'd insisted on Mercedes staying at his place this summer.

"You go over to see if she's home. I'm going to call Mercedes," Raul instructed.

Lorenzo was headed out the door before Raul could complete his sentence. He took his cell phone out of the top drawer of his desk and saw he had a voicemail from Mercedes. He hoped she was calling to tell him she was back, safely at his home.

"Hi, Raul, it's me. I'm just leaving Devyn's and got a call from Ron Sherman. He needs help with some work files before we start our training tomorrow with the rest of the staff. I'm going to head over to the school. I don't know how long I'll be, if you want to meet me there or I can just call when I'm on my way back home."

Raul listened to the message over again and a chill ran down his spine. It didn't feel right. He knew Mercedes was supposed to return to work the following day to begin the training and set up for the new school year, so why was Ron calling her to come in today?

Is Ron working with Rochelle to set Mercedes up? Raul grabbed his keys, his gun out of his office drawer, stuffed it in the back of his waist, and headed out the door.

Raul was so certain something was amiss, that on the way to his car, he called Lorenzo and diverted him to Mercedes' school instead of Rochelle's apartment. Raul tried to call Mercedes over and over again, but to no avail. Her phone was either on silent or she wouldn't or couldn't answer for some reason.

He hoped he wasn't too late. He immediately pushed those negative thoughts aside, knowing that he had to remain focused in order to help Mercedes.

CHAPTER 21

"Ron, are you here?" Mercedes yelled as she entered the dark outer office of the school.

The outer office was where the school's secretary sat, and there was a long bench for parents who were there to meet with the principal or assistant principals. Off to the right was Mercedes' own office along with the office for the other assistant principals. To the left was the larger principal's office. Mercedes found it strange that the lights in the outer office were off, but the lights in Ron's office were on.

"Ron, are you here?" she called again. She pushed through the small swinging door that stopped around mid-thigh, and that separated the parents' waiting area with the secretary and staff area. She stepped through the doorway and made her way to Ron's office.

She saw him sitting at his desk with an unreadable expression on his face.

When he saw her his eyes filled with relief and then worry, Mercedes felt the hairs at the back of her neck stand up.

"R-Ron, what's—"

"Hello, Mercedes," a cold voice welcomed her.

Mercedes didn't even notice the face of the person who the voice belonged to. She was too busy looking down the barrel of the gun that was now pointed at her. When she finally took her eyes off the gun and looked up into the face of the person who held the gun, she was shocked at who was there.

"Roxxy?" she gasped. "It's you? You're the—"

"Oh, no. Now is not the time for questions. In!" Rochelle insisted, waving the gun in the direction of Ron's office for Mercedes to enter.

"Sit!" she commanded, pointing at the chair across from Ron's desk.

At that time, Mercedes noticed that Ron's wrists had been duct taped to his chair.

'I'm sorry,' he mouthed to her as she looked at him.

She knew he was apologizing for being forced to make that call to her. Setting her up.

"Well, look who we have here. The famous Mercedes Holmes, or should I say Black Dahlia?" Rochelle asked loudly, arms flailing.

"Rochelle, what is this about? Why are you doing this?" Mercedes asked, trying to sound as calm as possible. She knew she had to keep her cool if she wanted to get the answers she needed and to make it out of this alive.

Mercedes found relief in knowing she had left that message for Raul.

"Why am I doing this? You really want to know, Black Dahlia?"

"Yes, I want to know what I did to you to make you hate me this much," Mercedes answered honestly. She could see the glossed over look in Roxxy's eyes. She knew the woman was not dealing with a full deck right now.

"Because you took everything from me!" Roxxy thrust the gun in Mercedes' face.

Mercedes flinched and her heartbeat thundered in her ears.

"If it wasn't for you, my life would be so different. Better," Roxxy screamed.

"I-I don't understand. What did I do?" Mercedes asked, confused.

"You were born!" Roxxy yelled hysterically. "If it wasn't for you, my father would be with me and my mother. I wouldn't have had to take care of her myself. I would've been able to be a kid, finish school, go to college. But no! You are the reason he wasn't around, so I had to do it all!"

Mercedes was still confused. She had no idea what Roxxy was talking about. Staring at Roxxy, she tried to make sense of what she was saying.

"You're father? I don't understand. What does your father have to do with me?"

"For an assistant principal of a school, you really are stupid, aren't you? You did a bang up job hiring this one," she derided Mercedes as she looked over at Ron who sat silently at his desk with a grim face.

He looked as confused as Mercedes felt.

"My father, or I should say *our* father, is one Dwayne Holmes, of Pearland, Texas," Roxxy said as she walked closer to Mercedes, bending so their faces were even with one another.

Mercedes looked into Roxxy's face. She noticed the eye color that mirrored her own, the similar skin complexion, and even the shape of Roxxy's nose—a physical trait Mercedes inherited from her father.

Realization began to settle in the pit of Mercedes' stomach.

Roxxy was her sister … her father's illegitimate daughter. Mercedes had even more questions now. How old was Roxxy? Where had she been? Who was her mother? And most important, why did Roxxy blame her for her father's absence?

"Roxxy—"

"Rochelle!" she yelled.

"Wh-What?" Mercedes asked.

"My name is Rochelle. I hate that fucking stage name!"

"Okay, Rochelle. I don't know what you think you know about me, but I had no idea you even existed." She tried to find some sort of connection with the woman. "If I had known I had a sister I would have sought you out."

"Oh, is that right?" Rochelle laughed sardonically. "You would have tried to find me? For what? So we could be a family? So we could be sisters?"

Mercedes could feel Rochelle's anger rising. She wanted to keep her calm for as long as possible. "Yes. I would have wanted that. I always wanted a sister. I'm sorry my ... our father wasn't there for you. He should have been—"

"Yes, he should have been! But because of you he wasn't! He loved my mother, but he told her he couldn't leave his bitch of a daughter. Even when he found out my mother was pregnant, he refused to leave his wife or you. He said he couldn't scandalize his church like that, so he turned his back on us. He chose you over us. It's your fault I grew up without a father!" Rochelle yelled and ranted.

Mercedes began to realize what Rochelle's rage was about. She blamed Mercedes for missing out on the life she thought she should have had growing up. Instead of putting her anger at her father's abandonment on him, she misdirected it at Mercedes, who was only a child herself when their father abandoned Rochelle and her mother.

Maybe she could reason with Rochelle.

"Rochelle, I'm so sorry you went through everything you did as a child. If I could change what our father did to you and your mother I would. He is not the perfect father you believe him to be. He's cheated on my mother for years. He has never been faithful. He may have told your mother he loved her, but he had many women he's said that to. He only loves himself," Mercedes told her truthfully.

The truth was her father came across as the preacher who was a doting husband and father, but looks could be deceiving. He used his position as a pastor to seduce women into confiding in and trusting him before bedding them.

Some of those women had even confronted Mercedes' mother over the years, but her mother refused to leave her husband, ever the dutiful wife and faithful servant.

"You're lying!" Rochelle shouted at her. "He loved my mother. She told me. It was you. You're the reason he stayed. You're the reason my father never saw me. Never reached out to get to know me. It was you!"

Mercedes could feel the woman spiraling out of control. She realized that trying to reason with Rochelle was out of the question. She'd probably spent years blaming Mercedes for something that was beyond her control. Mercedes would not be able to undo a lifetime of delusion in a few minutes. More importantly, Mercedes knew she only had mere minutes left if she didn't regain control of this situation.

Mercedes thought of trying another tactic. She'd use the first rule of capoeira that Raul had taught her; trickery and evasion.

"I'm sorry, Rochelle. You're right. It was me, I begged him to stay," she lied to the woman. "I saw him packing to leave one day and I couldn't let that happen. I needed my father. I didn't know he had another daughter though." Mercedes tried to sound sincere as she lied to Rochelle.

She hoped confessing to her own selfishness would mollify Rochelle in some way.

"I knew it!" Rochelle said, obviously satisfied with Mercedes' confession.

She began pacing back and forth.

"I knew it was you. My mother told me it was your fault ..." Rochelle continued to ramble to herself, pacing back and forth in the room.

Out of the corner of her eye, Mercedes saw movement. She turned her head slightly, to see Raul standing in the shadow of Ron's doorway. A wave of relief washed over Mercedes. She knew they weren't out of the woods yet, but knowing he was there gave her the added confidence that she needed to believe she'd make it out of this alive.

Raul nodded his head and put his finger over his lips, signaling for her to keep quiet and not draw attention to his presence. Mercedes turned to see Rochelle still pacing and mumbling to herself.

Mercedes looked to Ron, who still sat quietly, his face a mask of alarm and fear. Refocusing her attention on Rochelle, she could see the woman become even more unraveled right before her eyes. She continued to pace and mumble about knowing her father loved her and it was Mercedes' fault that he left her.

Mercedes got the eerie notion Rochelle was gearing herself up to finally end this, and not in the way Mercedes would want it to end.

Raul must have sensed the exact same thing, since once Rochelle paced in the opposite direction again, he made his move. Mercedes didn't see it coming, but she saw a flash of white in front of her, before she felt strong arms grip her and throw her down to the floor. Something heavy covered her face and body.

All she saw was darkness, but she could hear. She heard Rochelle screeching and a man grunting, before the loud "pow" of a gun went off. Mercedes could hear what sounded like someone or something heavy falling to the floor.

She tried to maneuver her body to see what was going on, but the body on top of hers wouldn't budge. Somehow, she instinctively knew it wasn't Raul who covered her.

She had come to know the feel and scent of his body on hers, and even in a life-or-death situation such as this, she knew that whoever was on top of her, it wasn't Raul. It felt like an eternity to Mercedes before the sounds quieted and the body on top of her shifted, easing their weight off her.

"You okay, boss?" Mercedes heard a voice ask. Despite her haze and confusion, she could make out Lorenzo's voice.

"Yeah, I'm fine." That was Raul.

Mercedes felt a hand grip hers, pulling her up to stand. She blinked a few times, turning in search of Raul. She first saw Ron standing behind his desk with a weary look on his face. He was fine.

She found Raul standing a few feet from Ron's desk, leering over Rochelle, who was now sitting on the floor with her hand handcuffed behind her back.

She appeared to be dazed.

"Raul!" Mercedes shouted, taking a few steps over to him and reaching out to throw her arms around him.

"Are you okay, querida?" he asked her as she buried her face into the crook of his neck.

She breathed deeply, caught between never wanting to leave his embrace and wanting to get answers to her remaining questions. The next words she heard caused her heart to leap into her throat.

"Shit, boss, you've been shot!"

Mercedes' head popped up from Raul's neck as soon as Lorenzo's words registered. "What?"

Pulling back, Mercedes saw the red stain that was growing larger by the second on Raul's white shirt. She gasped, her voice thick with fear and emotion. "Oh my God, Raul! You've been shot!"

CHAPTER 22

Two weeks later

"Thanks for coming, Jamal. I'm excited for you to get to know Raul." Mercedes hugged her brother as they prepared to sit down in her living room.

Jamal, having heard about everything Mercedes had gone through in the last couple of months, finally took his vacation time and came for a visit. Mercedes insisted he stay in her apartment, which she'd gotten newly refurbished, while she continued to stay at Raul's.

The trio had had dinner the previous night at Raul's home.

"Speaking of, how is he feeling? I'm surprised you left his side for this long. You've been attached to that man's hip since he left the hospital." Jamal joked.

It was true.

Upon learning Raul had been shot, Mercedes felt fear unlike any she'd ever felt before. He suffered a gunshot wound to the shoulder. Luckily, it wasn't life threatening, but it had done some damage to his muscle and arteries, so he required surgery, and there would be months of physical therapy to get him back to one hundred percent.

Mercedes had taken off the first couple of weeks of the school year, given what happened, and in order to tend to Raul.

He'd been home for the last two days and she was so grateful to have him home.

"Shut up." Mercedes playfully swatted at her brother. "He's doing well. His parents and Iris are with him at the house now, which is why I decided to come check in with you. I really appreciate you coming to visit," she told Jamal sincerely.

"Oh, please. You think I heard everything that happened and wouldn't get on the first thing smoking to make sure you were all right?" he asked, almost affronted.

"No, I knew you would, and I still appreciate it. I love you, bro."

"I love you, too, sis. So, tell me how you're really doing. It had to be a trip learning our father had an illegitimate daughter like that, and realizing that's who's been stalking you. That must be hard," Jamal said sympathetically.

Mercedes thought about it.

"Truthfully, what was hard was not knowing who was stalking me all these months and why. I mean, of course I was shocked to learn the truth, but once it all settled in, I was over the shock. It's not really a stretch to believe our father had at least one illegitimate child. As much as he's been stepping out on Mama over the years. I actually feel sorry for Rochelle," Mercedes said, shaking her head.

She'd developed a sense of sympathy since finding out the truth. The younger woman had had a hard life, growing up in Chicago with a sick mother. She directed her pain and resentment at Mercedes instead of the father her mother had taught her to hero worship.

Since that day in Ron's office, Rochelle had been arrested, and then taken to a mental institution after an evaluation found her incompetent to stand trial. Rochelle had been spiraling out of control for months, trying to sabotage Mercedes' life.

Once Raul thwarted her attempt to end Mercedes' life, she continued to rant and rave about her life being Mercedes' fault. Rochelle would probably spend years in that institution, if not the rest of her life. Mercedes was grateful it was all over with, but she still felt sympathy for the woman, and her anger with their father only grew.

"Yeah, I don't know about that, but I'm glad Rambo was there to save you."

Mercedes laughed.

Jamal had taken to calling Raul Rambo after learning his background and hearing he'd taken a bullet for his sister.

"You know Mama is moving in with Aunt Sheryl?" Jamal asked.

Mercedes nodded. "Mmhm, we talked a couple of days ago. She's going to come out for a while to visit once she gets settled in," Mercedes confirmed.

She'd had a long talk with her mother, who'd apologized for allowing her father to treat her so harshly growing up, and not being strong enough to leave him when she and Jamal were younger. Mercedes heard the pain and anguish in her mother's voice as they talked. She'd finally had enough.

It was one thing to have women confront her over the years, but now to have an illegitimate daughter threaten the life of her own daughter. Linda was done putting up a front for other people.

Mercedes was proud of her.

"Yeah, I helped her move. After I cursed Dad out." Mercedes could hear the thread of anger in Jamal's voice.

"You did what?"

"You heard me. Fuc— forget that man. What? You think you were the only one who heard Mama crying alone in her room all those nights? Nah, you weren't. I promised myself I'd never treat my woman like that, *if* I ever get married ... and that's a big if.

"Anyway, after what happened to you and Mama telling me what he said to you in New Orleans I lost it on him. I would never put my hands on my father, but after seeing the way he hurt the two most important women in my life, I was tight. I'm sorry I never said anything sooner, Mercedes. I wish I had stood up to him about this years ago," Jamal admitted, looking down at his hands as if he was ashamed.

Mercedes' heart swelled with love and gratitude for her younger brother. "Jamal, you have nothing to apologize for. That was all Dad's doing. He made his own bed, let him lay in it alone. You don't place the burden of shame on yourself."

Jamal continued to look down for a few moments, taking in what Mercedes just told him. Eventually he lifted his head, looking at Mercedes, and nodded. "Okay, so tell me about this Raul cat. You love him, don't you?" Jamal asked, not even trying to beat around the bush.

"Damn, just dive right in, huh? What makes you think it's love?" she asked.

"Oh, please, sis. I saw you doting all over him last night. You were acting like the man had major heart surgery or something. I've never seen you that way over anyone. So tell me, when's the wedding?" he asked, laughing as he dodged Mercedes' playful punches.

* * *

"Raul, where are you?' Mercedes called as she entered the house. She'd just returned from her visit with her brother.

"I'm here, querida," she heard his sexy voice as he bounded down the steps dressed in a pair of blue jeans and a T-shirt. Her heart raced as he approached her with that sexy glint in his eyes. With his good arm he pulled her into a warm kiss. She allowed herself to get lost in his kiss as their lips got reacquainted with one another.

"How's Jamal?" Raul asked when they finally broke apart.

"He's good. He told me he likes you," she told him.

"I'm sorry, querida … you'll have to tell him I'm flattered, but I'm taken," he joked.

Mercedes laughed and playfully slapped his arm.

"Anyway, smartass. Where are your parents and Iris?" she asked, looking over his shoulder to see if anyone was still around.

"They left. I had to shoo them out of here. I needed some time alone with my woman. Come," he said, tugging her hand and walking toward the back patio.

Mercedes stepped out to see a candlelight dinner had been set up on the table.

"Raul, you didn't do this yourself, did you?" she turned and asked.

"I had some help. Both mamas and even Papa helped," he told her.

Mercedes was relieved to hear he hadn't done all this by himself and risked further injury to his hurt shoulder.

As it stood, he often refused to wear the sling the hospital had given him, which he wasn't wearing now.

"And before you ask where my sling is, it's in the room. The doctor said I could spend a few hours a day out of it. Sit," he said, pulling out a chair.

Mercedes eyed him suspiciously.

"I want to make sure you're okay and not overdoing it," she defended her sometimes overprotective ways.

"I know, querida. That's just one of the reasons why I love you," he said casually, placing a kiss on her forehead.

The day Raul got shot, was also the first time he told Mercedes he loved her. It was on the way to the hospital in the ambulance as she held his hand. He'd managed to tell her every day since, and Mercedes still hadn't gotten tired of hearing it. She hadn't said the words yet, but she was ready to change that, after she confessed something first.

"What is all this for?" Mercedes asked.

"A token of my appreciation … and a little something else. You've barely left my side since I was in the hospital, and I am grateful."

Mercedes' heart smiled at his admission, but she felt a little guilty. "Well, I mean, it was my fault you were shot." She grabbed his hand across the table.

"There's so much I want to say. When I saw you had been shot and were bleeding, I nearly fainted. I was so scared you w-were …" She trailed off, not able to bring herself to say the words that she feared he could have died.

Raul consolingly brought her hand to his lips.

"Just please don't ever do that to me again. I need you around for a long time," she told him.

"How long?"

"As long as you'll have me," she answered sincerely. By the sexy smile that formed on Raul's lips, she knew her answer satisfied him.

"I need to tell you something about me that's important for you to know." Mercedes paused, waiting for his response.

When Raul nodded, she continued, "I don't know where to start. I mean, you've met my parents and you were nearly killed by my illegitimate sister, so you know how fucked up my family is. But I wouldn't be surprised if I had more siblings out there I don't know about. When I was eight years old, I remember being in a grocery store with my mother and a woman came up to us.

"I can't recall the entire conversation, but I remember the woman taunting my mother about how my father didn't love her and how he only stayed with her to keep up appearances.

"I mean, this woman was bold enough to do this right in front of me. My mother hurried us out of the store. Later that night, it was one of the only times I heard my parents argue. After all the yelling, my father hurried out of the house, barely looking at me. I remember going to bed to the sounds of my mother crying that night. After that, I promised myself I would never let myself fall for someone who could treat me the way my father treated my mother. I spent most of my life avoiding serious relationships because I didn't want to be vulnerable. And then you happened."

Mercedes stopped to catch her breath and let her words settle around them. "I don't want to be that way with you. You make me want more. What I'm trying to say is, I love you, Raul," she said with tears in her eyes.

She barely registered Raul's movement, before he was pulling her up out of her seat and into his arms. After a few heartbeats, Raul took a step back.

"I'm glad you said that, finally, because I have something I want to ask you." With his good arm, he reached into his pants pocket and pulled out a ring box.

Mercedes' eyes widened at the realization of what he held.

"Raul," she whispered, as he dropped down to one knee and held up the open ring box.

"I want you for as long as I have breath in my body. I promise to be faithful, loving, and to cherish you for as long as God allows me to. Marry me, querida?" he asked, his voice thick with emotion.

Mercedes looked at the sincerity in Raul's eyes and was reminded of how safe she always felt around him. How caring and loved she felt in his embrace. She knew she could trust Raul with her heart, for a lifetime. She knelt to the ground in front of him and nodded, too overcome with emotion to speak.

She held out her hand, and he slipped the cushion-cut Tiffany diamond onto her left ring finger. Mercedes threw her arms around his neck, making sure to be careful of his injured shoulder. She pressed her lips to his, meaning for the kiss to be brief, but Raul had other ideas.

He instantly deepened the kiss. Pulling back, he stood.

"Come with me, querida."

He brought her into the house and up the stairs. They spent the next few hours showing each other exactly how they felt for one another, having forgotten all about their uneaten dinner.

"Do you prefer a fall or a spring wedding?" Raul asked Mercedes that night as they lay in bed.

EPILOGUE

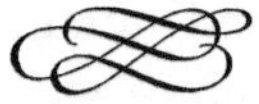

ine months later
"You take my breath away, Mrs. Santiago."

Mercedes smiled when she felt Raul's arms encircle her waist from behind. She leaned back into his chest as she looked out over the beautiful blue ocean of the Copacabana beach. The couple had married at the Copacabana hotel in Rio and opted to take their wedding photos out on the beach before returning for the reception.

Mercedes turned in his arms, facing her husband. "You stole mine a long time ago, Mr. Santiago," she said as she raised her tiptoes, pressing a kiss to his lips.

"Ready to go greet our guests?" he asked.

Mercedes nodded.

They returned to the vehicle to take them the short distance back to the hotel reception. They waited until Mercedes' school year ended to marry, so they would have more time to honeymoon in Brazil. The couple planned to spend most of the summer in Raul's native country.

He looked forward to showing his new wife his most cherished locations in his beloved country.

"Here they come!" shouted Mercedes' matron of honor, Devyn, who'd just given birth to a baby girl six weeks earlier.

Nikola and Devyn chose to name their new daughter Cassandra, and once again, Raul and Mercedes were the godparents. The guests cheered as the wedding party was announced, and stood as Raul and Mercedes were introduced as Mr. and Mrs. Raul Santiago.

Raul and Mercedes had their first dance to "At Last" by Etta James. The couple danced in the center of the reception hall, while their guests admired them, clapping once the song was over. For the next few hours they danced, partied, and celebrated with their friends and family.

"Congratulations, young lady." Mercedes turned from her conversation with Devyn to see Mistress Coco with a younger man who appeared to be her date.

"Thank you so much, Mistress Coco, and thank you for coming. I'm glad you could get someone to watch the club so you could make it down here," Mercedes stated.

Mistress Coco waved her off. "Chile, Iris has been trying to get me down here for forever. I'm glad I could make it! Now I have a chance to take advantage of the … view," she said as she mischievously eyed the six foot tall, chestnut-colored, bald-head man she had her arm wrapped around.

The man appeared to be in his mid-forties, some twenty years or so younger than Mistress Coco. And apparently, was a Brazilian native.

"Diane, I'm going to let you talk with your friends. I'll refresh your drink for you," he announced in his beautifully accented English before placing a kiss on Mistress Coco's cheek and strolling off.

Devyn and Mercedes eyed the man as he walked off and then one another.

"Young ladies, don't look so surprised. Who the hell do you think it was that taught Stella to get her groove back?" Mistress Coco asked them.

The trio laughed and talked for a few more minutes, before they were joined by Iris, Rosaline, and Mercedes' mother, Linda. Mercedes and her mother had worked on their relationship in the last nine months, and they were becoming closer than ever.

Linda had decided to follow through with a divorce from Dwayne, and she even began taking computer classes at a local community college. Mercedes was proud of her mother for taking control of her life. She promised to help in any way she could.

Dwayne was a different story altogether. He placed the blame for his divorce squarely on the shoulders of his wife, saying she wasn't loyal in the face of adversity.

While many members of his congregation continued to support him, others left after finding out about his infidelities and that he abandoned a daughter he had outside of his marriage. He had not spoken to Mercedes since he'd left New Orleans.

Mercedes was disappointed, but she refused to feel guilty over the sins of her father. And that day was one of the happiest days of her life. She was ready to celebrate with the man she loved.

* * *

"How's it feel to be married?" Nikola asked his best friend.

"It feels pretty damn good. You should have told me it felt this good. I might have done it sooner," Raul joked.

"Yeah, well count me out of that shit," Nikola's younger brother, Andre, said, approaching the two men.

Raul and Nikola stared at one another, knowing Andre could try to avoid it all he wanted, but when it was his time to fall, he'd fall as hard as they did. Both men also knew that Andre would be an even bigger challenge than they were.

Laid back as he came off, Andre could be the most stubborn out of the three men. He was no easy catch, but by the looks Iris, Mistress Coco, and even Rosaline were giving him, he'd meet his match soon, if they had anything to say about it.

"If you say so, junior," Raul said, clapping Andre on the back.

"Raul, Mercedes was asking for you," Stacey, one of Mercedes' bridesmaids, interrupted.

Mercedes and Stacey had become good friends over the last year.

Raul and Nikola both had noticed the sly looks Andre had sent Stacey's way when he thought no one was looking.

"Thank you, Stacey. I think it's about damn time I take my bride out of here anyway. If you'll excuse me," he said, departing from the group.

Raul glanced at the group of women off to the side of the room, and watched as a satisfied smile spread across Iris' face when she noticed the look Andre was giving Stacey.

Maybe sooner than later. Raul laughed to himself as he strolled off in search of his bride.

"I heard you were looking for me," he whispered in his wife's ear from behind. He spun her around and pressed a kiss to her lips before she could respond.

"Mmm," she moaned into his mouth. He reached around to grip a generous portion of the ass he loved so much.

Gasping, Mercedes pulled away. "Raul, you can't feel me up like that in front of all our guests."

"The hell I can't," he growled, pulling her to him once again.

Mercedes laughed.

"No, there are serious people here," she playfully retorted, wriggling in his arms.

"Fuck it then. It's time to go anyway," he said at the same time he hoisted Mercedes, wedding dress and all, over his shoulder and began strolling to the elevator door.

Their guests whooped and hollered at Raul's antics, drowning out Mercedes' protests.

"I'm going to kick your ass as soon as I get down from here," Mercedes threatened.

"Promises, promises." Raul laughed as he pressed the elevator button to take them up to their suite.

"Querida, tonight is only the beginning of the rest of our lives. And you can rest assured the only woman waiting in my room and in my bed tonight and forever will be you," he said as he placed Mercedes down in the elevator.

"Mm, sounds good to me." Mercedes sighed contentedly as her husband pressed kisses down her neck. That night would only be a prelude to the rest of their lives.

* * *

Click here to read Andre and Stacey's story in Black Butterfly.